To Hattie,

with a "Merry Christmas"

1896.

MARM LISA

BY

KATE DOUGLAS WIGGIN

The eternal-womanly
Ever leadeth us on.
Goethe's *Faust*.

BOSTON AND NEW YORK
HOUGHTON, MIFFLIN AND COMPANY
The Riverside Press, Cambridge
1897

The Riverside Press, Cambridge, Mass., U. S. A.
Electrotyped and Printed by H. O. Houghton & Co.

CONTENTS.

MARM LISA.

I.

EDEN PLACE.

EDEN PLACE was a short street running at right angles with Eden Square, a most unattractive and infertile triangle of ground in a most unattractive but respectable quarter of a large city. It was called a square not so much, probably, because it was triangular in shape as because it was hardly large enough to be designated as a park. As to its being called "Eden," the origin of that qualifying word is enveloped in mystery; but it is likely that the enthusiastic persons who projected it saw visions and dreamed dreams of green benches under umbrageous trees, of a green wire fence, ever green, and of plots of blossoming flowers filling the grateful air with unaccustomed fragrance.

As a matter of fact, the trees had always been stunted and stubby, the plants had

never been tended, and all the paint had
been worn off the benches by successive
groups of workingmen out of work.   As for
the wire fence, it had been much used as
a means of ingress and egress by the children of the neighborhood, who preferred it
to any of the gateways, which they considered hopelessly unimaginative and common-
place, offering no resistance to the budding
man of valor or woman of ambition.

Eden Place was frequented mostly by the
children, who found it an admirable spot to
squabble, to fight, and to dig up the hapless
earth, and after them, by persons out of
suits with fortune.   These (generally men)
adorned the shabby benches at all times,
sleeping, smoking, reading newspapers, or
tracing uncertain patterns in the gravel
with a stick, — patterns as uncertain and
aimless as themselves.   There were fewer
women, because the unemployed woman of
this class has an old-fashioned habit, or instinct, of seeking work by direct assault;
the method of the male being rather to sit
on a bench and discuss the obstacles, the
injustices, and the unendurable insults
heaped by a plutocratic government in the
path of the honest son of toil.

The corner house of Eden Place was a little larger than its neighbors in the same row. Its side was flanked by a sand-lot, and a bay window, with four central panes of blue glass, was the most conspicuous feature of its architecture. In the small front yard was a microscopic flower-bed; there were no flowers in it, but the stake that held up a stout plant in the middle was surmounted by a neat wooden sign bearing the inscription, "No Smoking on these Premises." The warning seemed superfluous, as no man standing in the garden could have put his pipe in his mouth without grazing either the fence or the house, but the owner of the "premises" possibly wished to warn the visitor at the very threshold.

All the occupied houses in Eden Place were cheerful and hospitable in their appearance, and were marked by an air of liveliness and good-fellowship. Bed linen hung freely from all the windows, for there was no hard-and-fast law about making up beds at any special hour, though a remnant of superstition still existed that it was a good thing to make up a bed before you slept in it. There were more women on their respective front steps, and fewer in their respective kitchens, in Eden Place than in almost any other locality in the city. That they lived for the most part in close and friendly relations could be seen from the condition of the fences between the front yards, whose upper rails fairly sagged with the weight of gossip.

One woman, living in the middle of the row, evidently possessed somewhat different views, for she had planted vines on each of her division fences, rented her parlor to a lodger who only slept there, kept all her front curtains drawn, and stayed in the back of her house. Such retribution as could legally be wreaked upon this offensive and exclusive person was daily administered by her two neighbors, who stood in their doors on either side and conversed across her house and garden with much freedom and exuberance. They had begged the landlord to induce her to take up her abode elsewhere, but as she was the only tenant who paid her rent regularly he refused to part with her.

Any one passing the "No Smoking" sign and entering the front door of Mrs. Grubb's house, on the corner, would have turned off the narrow uncarpeted hall into the principal room, and if he were an observing person would have been somewhat puzzled by its appearance. There were seven or eight long benches on one side, yet it had not the slightest resemblance to a schoolroom. The walls were adorned with a variety of interesting objects. There was a chart showing a mammoth human hand, the palm marked with myriads of purple lines. There were two others displaying respectively the interior of the human being in the pink-and-white purity of total abstinence, and the same interior after years of intemperance had done their fatal work; a most valuable chart this last, and one that had quenched the thirst of many a man.

The words *"Poverty Must Go"* were wrought in evergreen letters over the bay window, and various texts were printed in red and black and tacked to the wall in prominent places. These were such as:—

"To be a Flesh-Eater is to be a Shedder of Blood and a Destroyer of God's Innocent Creatures."

"Now that Man has Begun to Ascend in the Scale of Being let Woman Reach Down a Strong, Tender Hand and Aid him in his

Struggle for Moral and Spiritual Elevation."

"*Let the Pleasure Field be as Large as Possible. Pains and Fears Lessen Growth.*"

"*I Believe that to Burden, to Bond, to Tax, to Tribute, to Impoverish, to Grind, to Pillage, to Oppress, to Afflict, to Plunder, to Vampire the Life Laboring to Create Wealth, is the Unpardonable Sin.*"

Over the mantel-shelf was a seaweed picture in a frame of shells, bearing the inscription, "*Unity Hall. Meeting-Place of the Order of Present Perfection.*" On a table, waiting to be hung in place, was an impressive sort of map about four feet square. This, like many of the other ornaments in the room, was a trifle puzzling, and seemed at first, from its plenitude of colored spots, to be some species of moral propaganda in a state of violent eruption. It proved, however, on closer study, to be an ingenious pictorial representation of the fifty largest cities of the world, with the successful establishment of various regenerating ideas indicated by colored disks of paper neatly pasted on the surface. The key in the right-hand corner read: —

Temperance . . . . Blue.

Single Tax . . . . Green.

Cremation . . . . Orange.

Abolition of War . . Red.

Vegetarianism . . . Purple.

Hypnotism . . . . Yellow.

Dress Reform . . . Black.

Social Purity. . . . Blush Rose.

Theosophy . . . . Silver.

Religious Liberty . . Magenta.

Emancipation of Woman Crushed Strawberry.

A small gold star, added to the colored spot, hovering over the name of a city, was explained, in the lower left-hand corner, as denoting the fact that the Eldorado face powder was exclusively used there, and that S. Cora Grubb was the sole agent for the Pacific coast.

Joseph's coat faded into insignificance in comparison with the city of Mrs. Grubb's present residence, which appeared to be a perfect hot-bed of world-saving ideas, and was surrounded by such a halo of spots that it would have struck the unregenerate observer as an undesirable place in which to live, unless one wished to be broken daily on the rack of social progress.

This front room was Mrs. Grubb's only parlor. The seven benches were rather in the way and seemingly unnecessary, as the lady attended meetings morning, noon, and night in halls hired for that purpose; but they gave her a feeling of security, as, in case one of her less flourishing societies should be ejected from its hall, or in case she should wake up in the middle of the night and want to hold a meeting of any club when all the halls were closed, the benches in the parlor would make it possible without a moment's loss of time.

The room connecting with this was the family banquet-hall and kitchen in one, and as Mrs. Grubb's opinions on diet were extremely advanced, it amply served the purpose.

There were three bedrooms upstairs, and the whole establishment was rather untidy in its aspect; but, though it might have been much cleaner, it is only fair to say that it might also have been much dirtier.

The house was deserted. The only sound came from the back yard, and it was the echo of children's voices. It was not at all a merry prattle; it was a steady uproar interrupted by occasional shrieks and yells, a clatter of falling blocks, beatings of a tin pan, a scramble of feet, a tussle, with confusion of blows and thumps, and then generally a temporary lull in the proceedings, evidently brought about by some sort of outside interference. If you had pushed open the wire door, you would have seen two children of four or five years disporting themselves in a sand-heap. One was a boy and one a girl, and though they were not at all alike in feature or complexion, there was an astonishing resemblance between them in size, in figure, in voice, in expression, and, apparently, in disposition.

Sitting on a bench, watching them as a dog watches its master's coat, was a girl of some undeterminable age, — perhaps of ten or twelve years. She wore a shapeless stout gingham garment, her shoes were many sizes too large for her, and the laces were dangling. Her nerveless hands and long arms sprawled in her lap as if they had no volition in them. She sat with her head slightly drooping, her knees apart, and her feet aimlessly turned in. Her lower lip hung a little, but only a little, loosely. She looked neither at earth nor at sky, but straight at the two belligerents, with whose

bloodthirsty play she was obliged to interfere at intervals. She held in her lap a
doll made of a roll of brown paper, with a
waist and a neck indicated by gingham
strings. Pieces of raveled rope were pinned
on the head part, but there was no other
attempt to assist the imagination. She
raised her dull eyes; they seemed to hold in
their depths a knowledge of aloofness from
the happier world, and their dumb sorrow
pierced your very heart, while it gave you
an irresistible sense of aversion. She
smiled, but the smile only gave you a new
thrill; it was vacant and had no joy in it,
rather an uncommunicable grief. As she
sat there with her battered doll, she was to
the superficial eye repulsive, but to the eye
that pierces externals she was almost majes-
tic in her mysterious loneliness and separation.

The steam-whistle of a factory near by
blew a long note for twelve o'clock, and she
rose from her bench, took the children by
the hand, and dragged them, kindly but
firmly, up the steps into the kitchen. She
laid her doll under a towel, but, with a fur-
tive look at the boy, rolled it in a cloth and
tucked it under her skirt at the waist-line.

She then washed the children's faces, tied on their calico bibs, and pushed them up to the pine table. While they battered the board and each other with spoons and tin mugs, she went automatically to a closet, took a dish of cold porridge and turned it into three bowls, poured milk over it, spread three thick slices of wheat bread with molasses from a cup, and sat down at the table. After the simple repast was over, she led the still reluctant (constitutionally reluctant) twins up the staircase and put them, shrieking, on a bed; left the room, locking the door behind her in a perfunctory sort of way as if it were an every-day occurrence, crouched down on the rug outside, and, leaning her head back against the wall, took her doll from under her skirt, for this was her playtime, her hour of ease.

Poor little "Marm Lisa," as the neighbors called her! She had all the sorrows and cares of maternity with none of its compensating joys.

II.

MISTRESS MARY'S GARDEN.

" ' Mistress Mary, quite contrary,
　　How does your garden grow ? '
　' With silver bells and cockle shells,
　　And little maids all in a row.' "

MISTRESS MARY'S Garden did grow
remarkably well, and it was wonderfully
attractive considering the fact that few
persons beside herself saw anything but
weeds in it.

She did not look in the least a "contrary " Miss Mary, as she stood on a certain
flight of broad wooden steps on a sunshiny
morning; yet she was undoubtedly having
her own way and living her own life in spite
of remonstrances from bevies of friends,
who saw no shadow of reason or common
sense in her sort of gardening. It would
have been foolish enough for a young woman
with a small living income to cultivate roses
or violets or lavender, but this would at
least have been poetic, while the arduous

tilling of a soil where the only plants were little people "all in a row" was something beyond credence.

The truth about Mistress Mary lay somewhere in the *via media* between the criticisms of her skeptical friends and the encomiums of her enthusiastic admirers. In forsaking society temporarily she had no rooted determination to forsake it eternally, and if the incense of love which her neophytes forever burned at her shrine savored somewhat of adoration, she disarmed jealousy by frankly avowing her unworthiness and lack of desire to wear the martyr's crown. Her happiness in her chosen vocation made it impossible, she argued, to regard her as a person worthy of canonization; though the neophytes were always sighing to

> " have that little head of hers,
> Painted upon a background of pale gold."

She had been born with a capacity for helping lame dogs over stiles; accordingly, her pathway, from a very early age, had been bestrewn with stiles, and processions of lame dogs ever limping towards them. Her vocation had called her so imperiously that disobedience was impossible. It is all very

well if a certain work asks one in a quiet
and courteous manner to come and do it,
when one has time and inclination; but it
is quite another matter if it coaxes one so
insistently that one can do nothing else
properly, and so succumbs finally to the
persuasive voice. Still, the world must be
mothered somehow, and there are plenty of
women who lack the time or the strength,
the gift or the desire, the love or the patience, to do their share. This gap seems
to be filled now and then by some inspired
little creature like Mistress Mary, with
enough potential maternity to mother an
orphan asylum; too busy, too absorbed, too
radiantly absent-minded, to see a husband
in any man, but claiming every child in the
universe as her very own. There was never
anywhere an urchin so dirty, so ragged, so
naughty, that it could not climb into Mistress Mary's lap, and from thence into her
heart. The neophytes partook of her zeal
in greater or less degree, and forsaking all
probability of lovers (though every one of
them was young and pretty), they tied on
their white aprons and clave only unto her.
Daily intercourse with a couple of hundred
little street Arabs furnished a field for the

practice of considerable feminine virtue, and in reality the woman's kingdom at the top of the broad wooden steps was a great "culture engine" of spiritual motherhood.

It certainly was a very merry place, and if its presiding geniuses were engaged in conscious philanthropy the blighting hall-mark was conspicuous by its absence. Peals of laughter rang through the rooms; smiling faces leaned from the upstairs windows, bowing greeting to the ashman, the scissors-grinder, the Italian and Chinese vegetable-venders, the rag-sack-and-bottle man, and the other familiar figures of the neighborhood.

It was at the end of a happy, helpful day that Mistress Mary stood in the front door and looked out over her kingdom.

There was a rosy Swedish girl sitting on the floor of a shop window opposite and washing the glass. She had moved the fresh vegetables aside and planted herself in the midst of them. There she sat among the cabbages and turnips and other sweet things just out of the earth; piles of delicate green lettuce buds, golden carrots bursting into feathery tops, ruddy beets, and pink-cheeked potatoes. It was pretty to see the honest joy of her work and the interest of her parted lips, when, after polishing the glass, it shone as crystal clear as her own eyes. A milkman stopping to look at her (and small wonder that he did) poured nearly a quart of cream on the ground, and two children ran squabbling under the cart to see if they could catch the drippings in their mouths. They were Atlantic and Pacific Simonson, with Marm Lisa, as usual, at their heels. She had found her way to this corner twice of late, because things happened there marvelous enough to stir even her heavy mind. There was a certain flight of narrow, rickety steps leading to a rickety shanty, and an adjacent piece of fence with a broad board on top. Flower-pots had once stood there, but they were now lying on the ground below, broken into fragments. Marm Lisa could push the twins up to this vantage-ground, and crawl up after them. Once ensconced, if they had chosen the right time of day, interesting events were sure to be forthcoming. In a large playground within range of vision, there were small children, as many in number as the sands of the seashore. At a given moment, a lovely angel with black

hair and a scarlet apron would ring a large
bell. Simultaneously, a lovely angel with
brown hair and a white apron would fly to
the spot, and the children would go through
a mysterious process like the swarming of
bees around a queen. Slowly, reluctantly,
painfully, the swarm settled itself into lines
in conformance with some hidden law or
principle unknown to Marm Lisa. Then,
when comparative order had been evolved
from total chaos, the most beautiful angel
of all would appear in a window; and the
reason she always struck the on-lookers as
a being of beauty and majesty was partly,
perhaps, because her head seemed to rise
from a cloud of white (which was in reality
only a fichu of white mull), and partly because she always wore a slender fillet of
steel to keep back the waves of her fair
hair. It had a little point in front, and
when the sun shone on its delicate, fine-cut
prisms it glittered like a halo. After the
appearance of this heavenly apparition the
endless lines of little people wended their
way into the building and enchanting strains
of music were wafted through the open windows, supplemented sometimes by the inspiring rattle of drums and the blare of in-

struments hitherto indissolubly associated
with street parades.

Who? Why? Whence? Whither?
What for? These were some of the questions that assailed Marm Lisa's mind, but
in so incoherent a form that she left them,
with all other questions, unanswered. Atlantic and Pacific were curious, too, but
other passions held greater sway with them;
for when the children disappeared and the
music ceased, they called loudly for more,
and usually scratched and pinched Marm
Lisa as they were lifted down from the
fence; not seeing clearly how anybody else
could be held answerable for the cessation
of the entertainment, and scratches and
pinches being the only remedial agencies
that suggested themselves.

On this particular occasion there were no
bells, no music, and no mysterious swarming; but the heavenly apparition sat on the
broad steps. Yes, it was she! Blue-gray
eyes with darker lashes sweeping the warm
ivory of her cheeks, sweet true lips forever
parting in kind words, the white surplice
and apron, and the rememberable steel fillet. She had a little child in her lap (she
generally had, by the way), and there were

other tots clinging fondly to her motherly skirts. Marm Lisa stood at the foot of the steps, a twin glued to each side. She stared at Mistress Mary with open-mouthed wonder not unmixed with admiration.

"That same odd child," thought Mary. "I have seen her before, and always with those two little vampires hanging to her skirts. She looks a trifle young to have such constant family cares; perhaps we had better 'lend a hand.' "

"Won't you come in?" she asked, with a smile that would have drawn a sane person up the side of a precipice.

Atlantic turned and ran, but the other two stood their ground.

"Won't you come up and see us?" she repeated. "There are some fishes swimming in a glass house; come and look at them."

Marm Lisa felt herself dragged up the steps as by invisible chains, and even Pacific did not attempt to resist the irresistible. Atlantic, finding himself deserted by his comrades, gave a yell of baffled rage, and scrambled up the steps after them. But his tears dried instantly at the sight of the room into which they were ushered; as

large as any of the halls in which aunt Cora
spent her days, and how much more beautiful! They roved about, staring at the aqua-
rium, and gazing at the rocking-horse, the
piano, the drum, the hanging gardens, with
speechless astonishment. Lisa shambled at
their heels, looking at nothing very long;
and when Rhoda (one of the neophytes),
full of sympathy at the appearance of the
wild, forlorn, unkempt trio, sat herself
down on a sofa and gathered them about
a wonderful picture-book, Mistress Mary's
keen eyes saw that Lisa's gaze wandered in
a few minutes. Presently she crept over
the floor towards a table, and, taking a
string from it, began to blow it to and fro
as it hung from her fingers. Rhoda's glance
followed Mary's; but it was only a fleeting
one, for the four eyes of the twins were
riveted on hers with devouring eagerness,
while they waited for her explanation of the
pictures. At the end of half an hour, in
which the children had said little or nothing,
they had contrived to reveal so many sor-
rowful and startling details of their mental,
moral, and physical endowment that Mistress Mary put on her hat.

"I will go home with them," she said.

"There is plenty of work here for some-body; I could almost hope that it won't prove ours."

"It will," replied Rhoda, with a stifled sigh. "There is an old Eastern legend about the black camel that comes and lies down before the door of him upon whom Heaven is going to lay her chastening hand. Every time I have seen that awful trio on the fence-top, they were fairly surrounded by black camels in my imagination. Mis-tress Mary, I am not sure but that, in self-defense, we ought to become a highly spe-cialized *Something*. We are now a home, a mother, a nursery, a labor bureau, a divorce court, a registry of appeals, a soup kitchen, an advisory board, and a police force. If we take *her*, what shall we be?"

"We will see first where she belongs," smiled Mary. (Nobody could help smiling at Rhoda.) "Somebody has been neglect-ing his or her duty. If we can make that somebody realize his delinquencies, all the better, for the responsibility will not be ours. If we cannot, why, the case is clear enough and simple enough in my mind. We certainly do not want '*Mene, mene, tekel, upharsin*,' written over this, of all doors."

Rhoda's hand went up to an imaginary cap in a gesture of military obedience. "Very well, my general. I fly to prepare weapons with which to fight Satan. You, of course, will take *her;* oh, my dear, I'm almost afraid you ought n't! I choose the bullet-headed blonde twin who says his name is ' Lanty,' and reserve for Edith the bursting-with-fat brunette twin who calls herself ' Ciffy.' Edith's disciplinary powers have been too much vaunted of late; we shall see if Ciffy ruffles her splendid serenity."

III.

A FAMILY POLYGON.

MRS. GRUBB'S family circle was really
not a circle at all; it was rather a polygon,
— a curious assemblage of distinct personages.

There was no unity in it, no membership
one of another. It was four ones, not one
four. If some gatherer of statistics had
visited the household, he might have described it thus: —

"Mrs. S. Cora Grubb, widow, aged forty
years.

"Alisa Bennett, feeble-minded, aged ten
or twelve years.

"Atlantic and Pacific Simonson, twins,
aged four years."

The man of statistics might seek in vain
for some principle of attraction or cohesion
between these independent elements; but
no one who knew Mrs. Grubb would have
been astonished at the sort of family that
had gathered itself about her. Queer as it

undoubtedly was at this period, it had at
various times been infinitely queerer. There
was a certain memorable month, shortly
after her husband's decease, when Mrs.
Grubb allowed herself to be considered as
a compensated hostess, though the terms
"landlady" and "boarder" were never ut-
tered in her hearing. She hired a Chinese
cook, who slept at home, cleared out for the
use of Lisa and the twins a small storeroom
in which she commonly kept Eldorado face
powder, and herself occupied a sofa in the
apartment of a friend of humanity in the
next street. These arrangements enabled
her to admit an experimenter on hypnotism,
a mental healer who had been much abused
by the orthodox members of her cult and
was evolving a method of her own, an
ostensible delegate to an Occidental Confer-
ence of Religions, and a lady agent for a
flexible celluloid undershirt. For a few
days Mrs. Grubb found the society of these
persons very stimulating and agreeable, but
before long the hypnotist proved to be an
unscrupulous gentleman who hypnotized the
mental healer so that she could not heal,
and the Chinese cook so that he could not
cook. When, therefore, the delegate de-

parted suddenly in company with the cellu-
loid-underwear lady, explaining by a hurried postal card that they would "remit"
from Chicago, she evicted the other two
boarders, and retired again to private life.

This episode was only one of Mrs. Grubb's
many divagations, for she had been a person
of advanced ideas from a comparatively
early age. It would seem that she must
have inherited a certain number of "views,"
because no human being could have
amassed, in a quarter of a century, as many
as she held at the age of twenty-five. She
had then stood up with Mr. Charles Grubb
before a large assembly, in the presence of
which they promised to assume and continue
the relation of husband and wife so long as
it was mutually agreeable. As a matter of
fact it had not been mutually agreeable to
Mr. Grubb more than six months, but such
was the nobility of his character that he
never disclosed his disappointment nor
claimed any immunity from the responsibilities of the marriage state. Mr. Grubb was
a timid, conventional soul, who would have
given all the testimony of all the witnesses
of his wedding ceremony for the mere presence of a single parson; but he imagined

himself in love with Cora Wilkins, and she could neither be wooed nor won by any of the beaten paths that led to other women. He foolishly thought that the number of her convictions would grow less after she became a wife, little suspecting the fertility of her mind, which put forth a new explanation of the universe every day, like a strawberry plant that devotes itself so exclusively to "runners" that it has little vigor left for producing fruit.

The town in New York where they lived proving to be too small, narrow, and bigoted to hold a developing soul like Mrs. Grubb's, she persuaded her husband to take passage for California, where the climate might be supposed more favorable to the growth of saving ideas. Mr. Grubb would of course be obliged to relinquish his business, but people could buy and sell anywhere, she thought, and as for her, she wanted nothing but unlimited space in which to expand.

There was money enough for an economical journey and a month or two of idleness afterward, and as Mrs. Grubb believed everything in the universe was hers if she only chose to claim it, the question of finances never greatly troubled her. They sailed for the golden West, then, this ill-assorted couple, accompanied by Mrs. Grubb's only sister, who had been a wife, was now a widow, and would shortly become a mother. The interesting event occurred much sooner than had been anticipated. The ship became the birthplace of the twins, who had been most unwelcome when they were thought about as one, and entirely offensive when found to be two. The mother did not long survive the shock of her surprise and displeasure, and after naming the babies Atlantic and Pacific, and confiding them distinctly to the care of Mr., not Mrs., Grubb, she died and was buried at sea, not far from Cape Horn. Mrs. Cora enjoyed at first the dramatic possibilities of her position on the ship, where the baby orphans found more than one kindly sentimental woman ready to care for them; but there was no permanent place in her philosophy for a pair of twins who entered existence with a concerted shriek, and continued it forever afterward, as if their only purpose in life was to keep the lungs well inflated. Her supreme wish was to be freed from the carking cares of the flesh, and thus forever ready to wing her free spirit in the pure ether of speculation.

You would hardly suppose that the ob-
scure spouse of Mrs. Grubb could wash and
dress the twins, prepare their breakfast, go
to his work, come home and put them to
bed, four or five days out of every seven in
the week; but that is what he did, accept-
ing it as one phase of the mysterious human
comedy (or was it tragedy?) in which he
played his humble part.

Mrs. Grubb was no home spirit, no god-
dess of the hearth. She graced her family
board when no invitation to refresh herself
elsewhere had been proffered, and that she
generally slept in her own bed is as strong
a phrase as can be written on the subject.
If she had been born in Paris, at the proper
time, she would have been the leader of a
salon; separated from that brilliant destiny
by years, by race, and by imperious circum-
stance, she wielded the same sort of sceptre
in her own circumscribed but appreciative
sphere. No social occasion in Eden Place
was complete without Mrs. Grubb. With
her (and some light refreshment), a party
lacked nothing; without her, even if other
conditions were favorable, it seemed a flat,
stale, and unprofitable affair. Like Robin
Adair,

"She made the ball so fine :
She made th' occasion shine."

Mrs. Grubb hanging on her front gate, duster in hand (she never conversed quite as well without it, and never did anything else with it), might have been a humble American descendant of Madame de Staël talking on the terrace at Coppet, with the famous sprig of olive in her fingers. She moved among her subjects like a barouche among express wagons, was heard after them as a song after sermons. That she did not fulfill the whole duty of woman did not occur to her fascinated constituents. There was always some duller spirit who could slip in and "do the dishes," that Mrs. Grubb might grace a *conversazione* on the steps or at the gate. She was not one of those napkin people who hide their talents, or who immure their lights under superincumbent bushels. Whatever was hers was everybody's, for she dispensed her favors with a liberal hand. She would never have permitted a child to suffer for lack of food or bed, for she was not at heart an unkind woman. You could see that by looking at her vague, soft brown eyes, eyes that never saw practical duties straight in front of them, — liquid, star-gazing, vision-seeing eyes, that could never be focused on any near object, such as a twin or a cooking stove. Individuals never interested her; she cared for nothing but humanity, and humanity writ very large at that, so that once the twins nearly died of scarlatina while Mrs. Grubb was collecting money for the children of the yellow-fever sufferers in the South.

But Providence had an eye for Mr. Grubb's perplexities. It does not and cannot always happen, in a world like this, that vice is assisted to shirk and virtue aided to do its duty; but any man as marvelously afflicted as Mr. Grubb is likely to receive not only spiritual consolation, but miraculous aid of some sort. The spectacle of the worthy creature as he gave the reluctant twins their occasional bath, and fed them on food regularly prescribed by Mrs. Grubb, and almost as regularly rejected by them, would have melted the stoniest heart. And who was the angel of deliverance? A little vacant-eyed, half-foolish, almost inarticulate child, whose feeble and sickly mother was dragging out a death-in-life existence in a street near by. The child saw

Mr. Grubb wheeling the twins in a double perambulator; followed them home; came again, and then again, and then again; hung about the door, fell upon a dog that threatened to bite them, and drove it away howling; often stood over the perambulator with a sunshade for three hours at a time, without moving a muscle, and adored Mr. Grubb with a consuming passion. There was no special reason for this sentiment, but then Alisa Bennett was not quite a reasonable being. Mr. Grubb had never been adored before in his life; and to say the truth, his personality was not winning. He had a pink, bald head, pale blue eyes, with blonde tufts for eyebrows, and a pointed beard dripping from his chin which tended to make him look rather like an invalid goat. But as animals are said to have an eye for spirits, children have an eye for souls, which is far rarer than an eye for beautiful surfaces.

Mr. Grubb began by loathing Alisa, then patiently suffered her, then pitied, then respected, then loved her. Mrs. Grubb seldom saw her, and objected to nothing by which she herself was relieved of care. So Lisa grew to be first a familiar figure in the household, and later an indispensable one.

Poor Mrs. Bennett finally came to the end of things temporal. "Dying is the first piece of good luck I ever had," she said to Mr. Grubb. "If it turns out that I 've brought a curse upon an innocent creature, I 'd rather go and meet my punishment halfway than stay here and see it worked out to the end."

" ' In my Father's house are many mansions,' " stammered Mr. Grubb, who had never before administered spiritual consolation.

She shook her head. "If I can only get rid of this world, it 's all I ask," she said; "if the other one is n't any better, why, it can't be any worse! Feel under the mattress and you 'll find money enough to last three or four years. It 's all she 'll ever get, for she has n't a soul now to look to for help. That 's the way we human beings arrange things, — we, or the Lord, or the Evil One, or whoever it is; we bring a puzzle into the world, and then leave it for other people to work out — if they can! Who 'll work out this one? Who 'll work out this one? Perhaps she 'll die before the money's gone; let's hope for the best."

"Don't take on like that!" said Mr. Grubb despairingly, — "don't! Pray for resignation, can't you?"

"Pray!" she exclaimed scornfully. "Thank goodness, I've got enough self-respect left not to pray! — Yes, I must pray, I *must!* . . . Oh, God! I do not ask forgiveness for him or for myself; I only beg that, in some way I cannot see, we may be punished, and she spared!"

And when the stricken soul had fled from her frail body, they who came to prepare her for the grave looked at her face and found it shining with hope.

It was thus that poor little Alisa Bennett assumed maternal responsibilities at the age of ten, and gained her sobriquet of "Marm Lisa." She grew more human, more tract-able, under Mr. Grubb's fostering care; but that blessed martyr had now been dead two years, and she began to wear her former vacuous look, and to slip back into the past that was still more dreadful than the pre-sent.

It seemed to Mrs. Grubb more than strange that she, with her desire for freedom, should be held to earth by three children not flesh of her flesh, — and such children! The father of the twins had been a professional pugilist, but even that fact could never sufficiently account for Pacific Simonson. She had apparently inherited instincts from tribes of warlike ancestors who skulked behind trees with battleaxes, and no one except her superior in size and courage was safe from her violent hand. She had little wicked dark eyes and crimson swollen cheeks, while Atlantic had flaxen hair, a low forehead, and a square jaw. He had not Pacific's ingenuity in conceiving evil, but when it was once conceived, he had a dogged persistency in carrying it out that made him worthy of his twin.

Yet with all these crosses Mrs. Grubb was moderately cheerful, for her troubles were as nebulous as everything else to her mind. She intended to invent some feasible plan for her deliverance sooner or later, but she was much more intent upon development than deliverance, and she never seemed to have the leisure to break her shackles. Nothing really mattered much. Her body might be occasionally in Eden Place, but her soul was always in a hired

hall. She delighted in joining the New
Order of Something, — anything, so long
as it was an Order and a new one, — and
then going with a selected committee to
secure a lodge-room or a hall for meetings.
She liked to walk up the dim aisle with the
janitor following after her, and imagine
brilliant lights (paid for by collection), a
neat table and lamp and pitcher of iced
water, and herself in the chair as president
or vice-president, secretary or humble trus-
tee. There was that about her that pre-
cluded the possibility of simple membership.
She always rose into office the week after
she had joined any society. If there was
no office vacant, then some bold spirit (generally male) would create one, that Mrs.
Grubb might not wither in the privacy of
the ranks. Before the charter members
had fully learned the alphabet of their order
and had gained a thorough understanding
of the social revolution it was destined to
work, Mrs. Grubb had mastered the whole
scheme and was unfolding it before large
classes for the study of the higher theory.
The instant she had a tale to tell she pre-
sumed the "listening earth" to be ready to
hear it. The new Order became an old one

in course of time, and, like the nautilus, Mrs. Grubb outgrew her shell and built herself a more stately chamber. Another clue to the universe was soon forthcoming, for all this happened in a city where it is necessary only for a man to open his lips and say, "I am a prophet," and followers flock unto him as many in number as the stars. She was never disturbed that the last clue had brought her nowhere; she followed the new one as passionately as the old, and told her breathless pupils that their feet must not be weary, for they were treading the path of progress; that these apparently fruitless excursions into the domain of knowledge all served as so many milestones in their glorious ascent of the mountain of truth.

IV.

MARM LISA IS TRANSPLANTED.

It was precisely as Rhoda thought and feared. The three strange beings who had drifted within Mistress Mary's reach had proved to belong to her simply because they did not belong to anybody else. They did not know their names, the streets in which they lived, or anything else about which they were questioned, but she had followed them home to the corner house of Eden Place, although she failed, on the occasion of that first visit, to find Mrs. Grubb within. There was, however, a very voluble person next door, who supplied a little information and asked considerable more. Mrs. Sylvester told Mary that Mrs. Grubb was at that moment presiding over a meeting of the Kipling Brothers in Unity Hall, just round the corner.

"They meet Tuesdays and Thursdays at four o'clock," she said, "and you'd find it a real treat if you like to step over there."

"Thank you, I am rather busy this afternoon," replied Mary.

"Do you wish to leave any name or message? Did you want a setting?"

"A sitting?" asked Mary vaguely. "Oh no, thank you; I merely wished to see Mrs. Grubb — is that the name?"

"That's it, and an awful grievance it is to her, — Mrs. S. Cora Grubb. You have seen it in the newspapers, I suppose; she has a half column 'ad' in the Sunday Observer once a month. Wouldn't you like your nails attended to? I have a perfectly splendid manicure stopping with me."

"No, thank you. I hoped to see Mrs. Grubb, to ask if her children can come and spend the morning with me to-morrow."

"Oh, that'll be all right; they're not her children; she doesn't care where they go; they stay in the back yard or on the sand-lot most of the time; she's got something more important to occupy her attention. Say, I hope you'll excuse me, but you look a little pale. If you were intending to get some mental healing from Mrs. Grubb, why, I can do it; she found I had the power, and she's handed all her healing over to me. It's a new method, and is going to supersede all the others, we think. My hours are from ten to twelve, and two to four, but I could take you evenings, if you 're occupied during the day. My cures are almost as satisfactory as Mrs. Grubb's now, though I have n't been healing but six months last Wednesday."

"Fortunately I am very well and strong," smiled Mistress Mary.

"Yes, that 's all right, but you don't know how soon sickness may overtake you, if you have n't learned to cast off fear and practice the denials. Those who are living in error are certain to be affected by it sooner or later unless they accept the new belief. Why don't you have your nails done, now you 're here? My manicure has the highest kind of a polish, — she uses pumice powder and the rose of Peru lustre; you ought to try her; by taking twenty tickets you get your single treatments for thirty-five cents apiece. Not this afternoon? Well, some other time, then. It will be all right about the children, and very good of you to want them. Of course you can't teach them anything, if that 's your idea. Belief in original sin is all against my theories, but I confess I can't explain the twins without it. I sometimes wonder I can do any healing, with them in the next house throwing off evil influences. I am treating Lisa by suggestion, but she has n't responded any yet. Call again, won't you? Mrs. Grubb is in from seven to eight in the morning, and ten thirty to eleven thirty in the evening. You ought to know her; we think there 's nobody like Mrs. Grubb; she has a wonderful following, and it 's growing all the time; I took this house to be near her. Good-afternoon. By the way, if you or any of your friends should require any vocal culture, you could n't do better than take of Madame Goldmarker in number seventeen. She can make anybody sing, they say. I 'm taking of her right along, and my voice has about doubled in size. I ought to be leading the Kipling Brothers now, but my patients stayed so late to-day I did n't get a good start. Good-afternoon."

The weeks wore on, and the children were old friends when Mary finally made Mrs. Grubb's acquaintance; but in the somewhat hurried interviews she had with that lady at first, she never seemed able to establish the kind of relation she desired.

The very atmosphere of her house was chaotic, and its equally chaotic mistress showed
no sign of seeking advice on any point.

"Marm Lisa could hardly be received in
the schools," Mary told the listening neophytes one afternoon when they were all
together. "There ought of course to be a
special place for her and such as she, somewhere, and people are beginning to see and
feel the importance of it here; but until the
thought and hope become a reality the state
will simply put the child in with the idiots
and lunatics, to grow more and more
wretched, more hopeless, more stupid, until
the poor little light is quenched in utter
darkness. There is hope for her now, I
am sure of it. If Mrs. Grubb's neighbors
have told me the truth, any physical malady
that may be pursuing her is in its very first
stages; for, so far as they know in Eden
Place, where one doesn't look for exact
knowledge, to be sure, she has had but two
or three attacks ('dizziness' or 'faintness'
they called them) in as many years. She
was very strange and intractable just before
the last one, and much clearer in her mind
afterwards. They think her worse of late,
and have advised Mrs. Grubb to send her

to an insane asylum if she does n't improve. She would probably have gone there long ago if she had not been such a valuable watch-dog for the twins; but she does not belong there, — we have learned that from the doctors. They say decisively that she is curable, but that she needs very delicate treatment. My opinion is that we have a lovely bit of rescue-work sent directly into our hands in the very nick of time. All those in favor of opening the garden gates a little wider for Marm Lisa respond by saying ' Ay! ' "

There was a shout from the neophytes that shook the very rafters — such a shout that Lisa shuffled across the room, and sitting down on a stool at Mistress Mary's feet, looked up at her with a dull, uncomprehending smile. Why were those beloved eyes full of tears? She could not be displeased, for she had been laughing a moment before. She hardly knew why, but Mistress Mary's wet eyes tortured her; she made an ejaculation of discomfort and resentment, and taking the corner of her apron wiped her new friend's face softly, gazing at her with a dumb sorrow until the smile came back; then she took out her

string and her doll and played by herself as
contentedly as usual.

It was thus that heaven began to dawn
on poor Marm Lisa.   At first only a physical heaven : temporary separation from
Atlantic and Pacific; a chair to herself in
a warm, sunshiny room; beautiful, bright,
incomprehensible things hanging on the
walls; a soft gingham apron that her clumsy
fingers loved to touch; brilliant bits of color
and entrancing waves of sound that roused
her sleeping senses to something like pleasure; a smile meeting her eyes when she
looked up, — oh! she knew a smile, — God
lets love dwell in these imprisoned spirits!
By and by all these new sensations were
followed by thoughts, or something akin to
them.   Her face wore a brooding, puzzled
look.   "Poor little soul, she is feeling her
growing-pains!" said Mistress Mary.   It
was a mind sitting in a dim twilight where
everything seems confused.   The physical
eye appears to see, but the light never quite
pierces the dimness nor reflects its beauty
there.   If the ears hear the song of birds,
the cooing of babes, the heart-beat in the
organ tone, then the swift little messengers
that fly hither and thither in my mind and

yours, carrying echoes of sweetness unspeakable, tread more slowly here, and never quite reach the spirit in prison. A spirit in prison, indeed, but with one ray of sunlight shining through the bars, — a vision of duty. Lisa's weak memory had lost almost all trace of Mr. Grubb as a person, but the old instinct of fidelity was still there in solution, and unconsciously influenced her actions. The devotion that first possessed her when she beheld the twins as babies in the perambulator still held sway against all their evil actions. If they plunged into danger she plunged after them without a thought of consequences. There was, perhaps, no real heroism in this, for she saw no risks and counted no cost; this is what other people said, but Mistress Mary always thought Marm Lisa had in her the stuff out of which heroes and martyrs are made. She had never walked in life's sunny places; it had always been the valley of the shadow for her. She was surrounded by puzzles, with never any answer to one of them, but if only she had comprehended the truth, it was these very puzzles that were her salvation. While her feeble mind stirred, while it wondered, brooded, suffered, — though it did all these too seldom, — it kept itself alive, even if the life were only like the flickering of a candle. And now the candle might flicker, but it should never go out altogether, if half a dozen pairs of women's hands could keep it from extinction; and how patiently they were outstretched to shield the poor apology for a flame, and coax it into burning more brightly!

"Let the child choose her own special teacher," said Mistress Mary; "she is sure to have a strong preference."

"Then it will be you," laughed Helen.

"Don't be foolish; it may be any one of us, and it will prove nothing in any case save a fancy that we can direct to good use."

"She seldom looks at anybody but you," said Edith.

"That is true," replied Mary thoughtfully. "I think she is attracted by this glittering steel thing in my hair. I am going to weave it into Helen's curly crop some day, and see whether she misses it or transfers her affection. I have made up my mind who is the best teacher for her and whom she will choose."

Rhoda gave a comical groan. "Don't say it's I," she pleaded. "I dread it. Please, I am not good enough, I don't know how; and besides, she gives me the creeps!"

Mistress Mary turned on Rhoda with a reproachful smile, saying, "You naughty Rhoda, with the brightest eyes, the swiftest feet, the nimblest fingers, the lightest heart among us all, why do you want to shirk?"

Mistress Mary had noted the fact that Lisa had refused to sit in an unpainted chair, but had dragged a red one from another room and ensconced herself in it, though it was uncomfortably small.

Now Rhoda was well named, for she was a rose of a girl, with damask cheeks that glowed like two Jacqueminot beauties. She was much given to aprons of scarlet linen, to collars and belts of red velvet, and she had a general air of being fresh, thoroughly alive, and in a state of dewy and perennial bloom. Mary was right in her surmise, and whenever she herself was out of Lisa's sight or reach the child turned to Rhoda instinctively and obeyed her implicitly.

V.

HOW THE NEW PLANT GREW.

"Now, Rhoda dear," said Mistress Mary
one day, when Lisa had become somewhat
wonted to her new surroundings, "you are
to fold your hands respectfully in your lap,
and I will teach you things, — things which
you in your youth and inexperience have
not thought about as yet. The other girls
may listen, too, and catch the drippings of
my wisdom. I really know little about the
education of defective children, but, thank
Heaven, I can put two and two together, as
Susan Nipper said. The general plan will
be to train Lisa's hands and speak to her
senses in every possible way, since her or-
gans of sense are within your reach, and
those of thought are out of it. The hardest
lesson for such a child to learn is the subor-
dination of its erratic will to our normal
ones. Lisa's affection is the most hopeful
thing about her, and encourages me more
than anything else. It is not as if there

were no mental processes existing; they are
there, but in a very enfeebled state. Of
course she should have been under skilled
teaching the last six years, but, late as it
is, we could not think of giving up a child
who can talk, use her right hand, dress herself, go upon errands, recognize colors,
wash dishes; who is apparently neither vi-
cious nor cunning, but who, on the contrary,
has lived four years under the same roof
with Mrs. S. Cora Grubb without rebellion
or violence or treachery! Why, dear girls,
such a task, if it did not appeal to one on
the moral, certainly would on the intellectual side. Marm Lisa will teach us more in
a year, you may be sure, than we shall
teach her. Let us keep a record of our
experiments; drop all materials that seem
neither to give her sensations nor wake her
discriminative power, and choose others that
speak to her more clearly. Let us watch
her closely, both to penetrate the secret of
her condition and to protect the other children. What a joy, what a triumph, to say
to her some dear day, a few years hence,
' You poor, motherless bairn, we have swept
away the cobwebs of your dreams, given
you back your will, put a clue to things in

your hand: now go on and learn to live and be mistress of your own life under God!'"

It was at such a moment, when Mary's voice trembled and her eyes shone through a mist of tears like two victorious stars, that a hush fell upon the little group, and the spirit of the eternal child descended like a dove, its pure wings stirring the silence of each woman's heart. At such a moment, their daily work, with its round of harsh, unlovely, beautiful, discouraging, hopeful, helpful, heavenly duties, was transfigured, and so were they. The servant was transformed by the service, and the service by the servant. They were alone together, each heart knit to all the others by the close bond of a common vocation; and though a heretofore unknown experience, it seemed a natural one when Mistress Mary suddenly bent her head and said softly: —

"Father in heaven, it is by the vision of thy relation to us that we can apprehend our relation to these little ones. As we have accepted that high trust, so make us loyal to it. When our feet grow weary and our faith grows dim, help us to follow close after the ever perfect One who taught

even as we are trying to teach. He it was
whom the common people heard gladly.
He it was who disdained not the use of
objects and symbols, remembering it was
the childhood of the race. He it was who
spake in parables and stories, laying bare
soul of man and heart of nature, and reveal-
ing each by divine analogy. He it was
who took the little ones in his arms and
blessed them; who set the child in the
midst, saying, ' Except ye become as one of
these.' May the afterglow of that inspired
teaching ever shine upon the path we are
treading. May we bathe our tired spirits
in its warmth and glory, and kindle our
torches at the splendor of its light. We
remember that he told us to feed his lambs.
Dear Lord, help all the faithful shepherds
who care for the ninety-and-nine that lie in
the safe cover of the fold; help us, too, for
we are the wandering shepherds whose part
it is to go out over the bleak hills, up the
mountain sides and rocky places, and gather
in out of the storm and stress of things all
the poor, unshepherded, wee bit lammies
that have either wandered forlornly away
from shelter, or have been born in the wil-
derness and know no other home. Such an

one has just strayed into the fold from the
dreary hill-country. It needs a wiser shep-
herd than any one of us. Grant that by
gentleness, patience, and insight we may
atone somewhat for our lack of wisdom and
skill. We read among thy mysteries that
the divine Child was born of a virgin.
May he be born again and born daily in
our hearts, already touched by that remembrance and consecrated by its meaning.
And this we ask for love's sake. Amen."

Then there was a space of silence, — one
of those silences in which we seem to be
caught up into the heart of things, when
hidden meanings are revealed, when the
soul stretches itself and grows a little.

It was a few minutes later when Rhoda
said: "I am fired with zeal, I confess it.
Henceforth my single aim shall be to bring
Marm Lisa into her lost kingdom and in-
heritance. But meanwhile, how, oh how
shall I master the hateful preliminaries?
How shall I teach her to lace her shoes and
keep them laced, unless I invent a game for
it? How shall I keep her hair from dangling in her eyes, how keep her aprons neat?
— though in those respects she is no worse
than Pacific Simonson. I promised her a

doll yesterday, and she was remarkably good. Do you object, Mistress Mary?"

"I don't know how much rewards are used in these cases," answered Mary, "but why do you begin with them when the problem presents no insuperable difficulties as yet? Whenever she conquers herself, her awkward hands, her weak will, her inattention, her restlessness, give her some task she likes, some pleasure or occupation for which she has shown decided preference, and thus make happiness follow close upon the heels of effort. We who see more clearly the meaning of life know that this will not always happen, and we can be content to do right for right's sake. I don't object to your putting hosts of slumbering incentives in Lisa's mind, but a slumbering incentive is not vulgar and debasing, like a bribe."

A plant might be a feeble and common thing, yet it might grow in beauty and strength in a garden like Mistress Mary's. Such soil in the way of surroundings, such patient cultivation of roots and stems, such strengthening of tendrils on all sorts of lovely props, such sunshine of love, such dew of sympathy, such showers of kindness,

such favoring breezes of opportunity, such
pleasure for a new leaf, joy for a bud, gratitude for a bloom! What an atmosphere in
which to grow towards knowledge and goodness! Was it any wonder that the little
people "all in a row" responded to the
genius of Mistress Mary's influence? They
used to sing a song called The Light Bird,
in which some one, all unknown to the children, would slip into the playground with
a bit of broken looking-glass, and suddenly
a radiant fluttering disk of light would
appear on the wall, and dance up and down,
above and below, hither and yon, like a
winged sunbeam. The children held out
longing arms and sang to it coaxingly.
Sometimes it quivered over Mistress Mary's
head, and fired every delicate point of her
steel tiara with such splendor that the Irish
babies almost felt like crossing themselves.
At such times, those *deux petits cœurs secs*,
Atlantic and Pacific, and all the other full-
fledged and half-fledged scapegraces, forgot
to be naughty, and the millennium was fore-
shadowed. The neophytes declared Mistress Mary a bit of a magician. Somehow
or other, the evil imps in the children
shrank away, abashed by the soft surprise

of a glance that seemed to hope something
better, and the good angels came out of
their banishment, unfolded their wings, and
sunned themselves in the warmth of her
approving smile. Her spiritual antennæ
were so fine, so fine, that they discerned the
good in everything; they were feeling now
after the soft spot in the rocky heart of
Atlantic Simonson; they had not found it
yet, but they would, — oh, they would in
time; for if hope is the lover's staff, it is
no less that of the idealist.

Marm Lisa looked upon the miracles
that happened under Mistress Mary's roof
with a sort of dazed wonder, but her intelli-
gence grew a little day by day; and though
she sadly taxed everybody's patience, she
infused a new spirit into all the neophytes.

Had not improvement been rapid, their
untrained zeal might perhaps have flagged.
Had the mental symptoms, by their obscur-
ity, baffled them or defied them on every
side, their lack of systematic, scientific
training for such a task might have made
them discouraged; but delicate and exact-
ing as the work was, their love and enthusiasm, their insight and patience, their
cleverness and ingenuity, triumphed over

all obstacles; and luckily for their youth
and comparative inexperience, they were
rewarded in marvelous measure.

Not that every day was bright and hopeful. The carefully kept record was black
enough on occasions, beginning with the
morning when Helen, sitting in the circle,
felt a rough hand on her head, and Marm
Lisa, without the slightest warning of her
intention, snatched Mary's steel band forcibly from her hair, and taking it across the
room, put it in its accustomed place on its
owner's head. Everybody was startled,
but Mary rose from her chair quietly, and
taking the ornament in one hand and Marm
Lisa by the other, she came to Helen's side.

"I like to have my shining crown in Miss
Helen's hair," she said; "it is such pretty
curly hair, — stroke it softly, Lisa; she
must wear it this morning to please me, and
then I will take it again for my own. Dear
Miss Helen, who is so sweet and good to
the children, I love her," and she kissed
her fondly on each cheek.

Marm Lisa did not attempt to rebel, but
she was sullen, and refused her work when
it was offered her later.

Such occurrences were rare, however, for

her obliquity always seemed mental rather than moral.

Straws and bright papers, beads and pretty forms to thread on stout laces, were given her to wean her from her favorite but aimless string-play. There were days of restlessness, when she wandered up and down stairs, and could not be kept in her chair nor persuaded to stand in her place in the circle. There were days, too, when she tore the bright cardboards and glossy weaving mats that ordinarily gave her such keen pleasure; but this carelessness grew more and more infrequent until it ceased altogether, so that it had probably come more from her inability to hold and move the materials and needles properly than from a wanton instinct of destruction; for they would often see the tears drop from her eyes upon her clumsy fingers as she strove to make them obey her feeble behests. At such a moment there was always some one to fling herself with passionate ardor and sympathy into this latest difficulty. A stouter weaving-needle was invented, and a mat of pretty colored morocco substituted for the fragile paper; while the poor inert hands were held and coaxed and strengthened every day by finger gymnastics.

As Lisa grew in power Rhoda grew in ingenuity, and failure in any one particular only stimulated her genius of invention the more. Did she spill paste, mucilage, water, on her gingham aprons, and wipe anything and everything on them that came in her way, Rhoda dressed her in daintier ones of white cambric, with a ruffle at the neck and sleeves; the child's pleasure knew no bounds, and she kept the aprons clean. With Mrs. Grubb's permission her hair was cut shorter, and brushed back under a round comb. No regiment of soldiers could have kept the comb in place. It was taken away, and a blue ribbon substituted. She untied the ribbon every five minutes for two days, when Mary circumvented her by sewing a blue ribbon on each sleeve. This seemed to divert her attention from the head-band, and after a week or two she allowed it to remain without interference. Mary gave her low shoes, hoping that the lessened trouble of lacing them would make the task a possibility. There was no improvement. If she laced them, it was only under supervision, and they were always untied within the hour, the dangling laces tripping her awkward feet. Slippers or old-fashioned shoes with elastic at the side would have been an easy way out of the difficulty, but to Rhoda's mind that would have been a humiliating confession of failure. As a last resort she bought brown shoes and brown laces.

"If these do not succeed," she said, "I will have red ones made, paint the tips blue, and give her yellow laces; but I will fix her mind on her feet and arouse her pride in them, or die in the attempt."

This extreme, fortunately, proved unnecessary, since for some unknown reason the brown foot-gear appealed to Marm Lisa, and she kept the laces tied. The salient peculiarity and encouraging feature of the child's development was that, save in rare cases, she did not slip back into her old habits when the novelty of the remedy wore off ; with her, almost every point gained was a point kept. It was indeed a high Hill Difficulty that she was climbing, — so high that had she realized it she would never have taken the first step of her own unaided will; but now the impelling force behind her was so great, and the visions forever leading her on were so beautiful, that she ran nor grew weary, she walked yet did not faint.

The other children, even the youngest of them, were more or less interested in the novel enterprise, too, though they scarcely knew the nature of it or how much was at stake. That a human mind was tottering to its fall, and that Mistress Mary was engaged in preventing it, was beyond their ken. They could see certain details, however, for they were all one great family of little people, and it was no unaccustomed thing for them to watch a moral conquest, though they had no conception of an intellectual one.

Accordingly, there was a shout of triumph from a corner of the room one morning, — such a shout that seventy or eighty youngsters held their breath to see what was happening.

After weeks upon weeks of torn cards, broken threads, soiled patterns, wrong stitches, weak hand held in place by strong hand, Marm Lisa had sewed without help, and in one lesson, the outline of a huge red apple; and there she stood offering her finished work to Mistress Mary! The angels in heaven never rejoiced more greatly over the one repentant sinner than the tired shepherdesses over their one poor ewe lamb as she stood there with quivering hands and wet eyes, the first sense of conscious victory written on her inscrutable brow, and within the turbid, clouded brain the memory of a long struggle, and a hint, at least, of the glory she had achieved.

Rhoda took the square of neat cardboard with the precious red circle that meant so much, and ran into the playground with it, hugging it to her heart, and crying and laughing over it like a child.

When she came back, Mistress Mary put her arm round Lisa's waist and said to the whole great family: "Children, after trying hard for ever so long, Lisa has sewed this lovely picture all by herself. There is not a wrong stitch, and one side is as neat as the other. What shall we say?"

"Three cheers! The Chinese must go!" shouted Pat Higgins, a patriotic person of five years whose father was an organizer of sand-lot meetings.

All the grown-ups laughed at this unexpected suggestion, but the cheers were given with a good will, and Marm Lisa, her mind stirred to its depths by the unwonted emotion, puzzled out the meaning of them and hid it in her heart.

VI.

FROM GRUBB TO BUTTERFLY.

THE children were all nearly a year older
when Mrs. Grubb one day climbed the
flight of wooden steps leading to Marm
Lisa's Paradise, and met, as she did so, a
procession of Mistress Mary's neophytes
who were wending their way homeward.

The spectacle of a number of persons of
either sex, or of both sexes, proceeding in
line or grouped as an audience, acted on
Mrs. Grubb precisely as the taste of fresh
blood is supposed to act on a tiger in cap-
tivity. At such a moment she had but one
impulse, and that was to address the meeting. The particular subject was not vital,
since it was never the subject, but her own
desire to talk, that furnished the necessary
inspiration. While she was beginning,
"Ladies and gentlemen," in her clear, pleasant voice, her convictions, opinions, views,
prejudices, feelings, experiences, all flew
from the different corners of what she was

pleased to call her brain, and focused themselves on the point in question.

If the discussion were in a field in which she had made no excursions whatever, that trifling detail did not impose silence upon her. She simply rose and said: "Ladies and gentlemen, though a stranger in your midst, I feel I must say a word of sympathy to you, and a word of encouragement for your cause. It is a good and worthy movement, and I honor you for upholding it. Often and often have I said to my classes, it matters not what face of truth is revealed to you so long as you get a vision that will help you to bless your fellow men. To bless your fellow men is the great task before each and every one of us, and I feel to urge this specially upon occasions like this, when I see a large and influential audience before me. Says Rudyard Kipling, 'I saw a hundred men on the road to Delhi, and they were all my brothers.' Yes, all our brothers! The brotherhood of man and the sisterhood of woman, those are the subjects that include all others. I am glad to have met with you and to have heard the eloquent words of your speakers. If any of you would like to know more of my work, I will gladly meet you in room A at the close of this meeting."

She then sat down amid applause. Never did Mrs. S. Cora Grubb cease speaking without at least a ripple of approval that sometimes grew into a positive ovation. What wonder, then, that she mistook herself for an inspired person? It was easy to understand her popularity with her fellow men. Her eyes were as soft and clear as those of a child, her hair waved prettily off her low serene brow, her figure was plump and womanly, and when her voice trembled with emotion (which in her was a shallow well very near the surface) the charmingest pink color came and went in her cheeks. On such occasions more than one member of the various brotherhoods thought what a cosy wife she would make, if removed from the public arena to the "sweet safe corner of the household fire." To be sure she had not much logic, but plenty of sentiment; rather too great a fondness for humanity, perhaps, but that was because she had no husband and family of her own to absorb her superfluous sympathy and energy. Mrs. Grubb was not so easily classified as these "brothers" imagined, however, and fortunately for them she had no leanings towards any man's fireside. Mr. Grubb had died in the endeavor to understand her, and it is doubtful whether, had he been offered a second life and another opportunity, he would have thought the end justified the means.

This criticism, however, applies only to the family circle, for Mrs. Grubb in a hall was ever winning, delightful, and persuasive. If she was illogical, none of her sister women realized it, for they were pretty much of the same chaotic order of mind, though with this difference: that a certain proportion of them were everywhere seeking reasons for their weariness, their unhappiness, their poverty, their lack of faith and courage, their unsatisfactory husbands and their disappointing children. These ladies were apt to be a trifle bitter, and much more interested in Equal Suffrage, Temperance, Cremation, and Edenic Diet than in subjects like Palmistry, Telepathy, and Hypnotism, which generally attracted the vague, speculative, feather-headed ones. These discontented persons were always the most frenzied workers and the most eloquent speakers, and those who were deter-

mined to get more rights were mild com-
pared with those who were determined to
avenge their wrongs. There was, of course,
no unanimity of belief running through all
these Clubs, Classes, Circles, Societies,
Orders, Leagues, Chapters, and Unions;
but there was one bond of aversion, and
that was domestic service of any kind. That
no woman could develop or soar properly,
and cook, scrub, sweep, dust, wash dishes,
mend, or take care of babies at the same
time,— to defend this proposition they would
cheerfully have gone to the stake. They
were willing to concede all these sordid tasks
as an honorable department of woman's
work, but each wanted them to be done by
some other woman.

Mrs. Grubb really belonged to neither of
these classes. She was not very keen about
more rights, nor very bloodthirsty about
her wrongs. She inhabited a kind of serene
twilight, the sort that follows an especially
pink sunset. She was not wholly clear in
her mind about anything, but she was entirely hopeful about the world and its disposition to grow and move in ever ascending
spirals. She hated housework as much as
any of her followers, although she was sel-

dom allowed to do anything for herself. "I'll step in and make your beds, Mrs. Grubb; I know you're tired." "I'll sweep the front room, Mrs. Grubb; you give yourself out so, I know you need rest." "Let me cook your supper while you get up strength for your lecture; there are plenty of people to cook, but there's only one Mrs. Grubb!" These were the tender solicitations she was ever receiving.

As for theories, she had small choice. She had looked into almost every device for increasing the sum of human knowledge and hastening the millennium, and she thought them all more or less valuable. Her memory, mercifully, was not a retentive one, therefore she remembered little of the beliefs she had outgrown; they never left even a deposit in the stretch of wet sand in which they had written themselves.

She had investigated, or at any rate taught, Delsarte, Physical Culture, Dress-Reform, the Blue-glass Cure, Scientific Physiognomy, Phrenology, Cheiromancy, Astrology, Vegetarianism, Edenic Diet, Single Tax, Evolution, Mental Healing, Christian Science, Spiritualism, Theosophy, and Hypnotism. All these metamorphoses of thought had Mrs. S. Cora Grubb passed through, and was not yet a finished butterfly. Some of the ideas she had left far behind, but she still believed in them as fragments of truth suitable for feeble growing souls that could not bear the full light of revelation in one burst. She held honorary memberships in most of the outgrown societies, attended annual meetings of others, and kept in touch with all the rest by being present at their social reunions.

One of her present enthusiasms was her "Kipling Brothers," the boys' band enlisted under the motto, "I saw a hundred men on the road to Delhi, and they were all my brothers." She believed that there was no salvation for a boy outside of a band. Banded somehow he must be, then badged, beribboned, bannered, and by-lawed. From the moment a boy's mother had left off her bye-lows, Mrs. Grubb wanted him put under by-laws. She often visited Mistress Mary with the idea that some time she could interest her in one of her thousand schemes; but this special call was to see if the older children, whose neat handiwork she had seen and admired, could embroider mottoes on cardboard to adorn the Kipling room at an approaching festival. She particularly wanted "Look not upon the Wine" done in blood-red upon black, and "Shun the Filthy Weed" in smoke-color on bright green. She had in her hand a card with the points for her annual address noted upon it, for this sort of work she ordinarily did in the horse-cars. These ran: —

1st. Value of individuality. "*I* saw."

2d. Value of observation. "I *saw*."

3d. Value of numbers. "I saw a *hundred* men."

4th. Importance of belonging to the male sex. It was *men* who were seen on the road.

5th. What and where is Delhi?

6th. Description of the road thither.

7th. Every boy has his Delhi.

8th. Are you "on the road?"

9th. The brotherhood of man.

10th. The Kipling Brothers' Call to Arms.

She intended to run through the heads of this impassioned oration to Mistress Mary, whom she rather liked; and, in truth, Mary had difficulty in disliking her, though she thoroughly disapproved of her. She was so amiable, and apparently so susceptible to

teaching, that Mary always fancied her on
the verge of something better. Her vagaries, her neglects, and what to Mary's mind
were positive inhumanities seemed in a way
unconscious. "If I can only get into sufficiently friendly relations," thought Mary,
"so that I can convince her that her first
and highest duty lies in the direction of the
three children, I believe she will have the
heroism to do it!" But in this Mistress
Mary's instinct was at fault. Mrs. Grubb
took indeed no real cognizance of her immediate surroundings, but she would not have
wished to see near duties any more clearly.
Neither had she any sane and healthy interest in good works of any kind; she simply
had a sort of philanthropic hysteria, and
her most successful speeches were so many
spasms.

VII.

THE COMET AND THE FIXED STAR.

"I DON'T feel that I can part with Lisa now, just as she's beginning to be a help to me," argued Mrs. Grubb, shortly after she had been welcomed and ensconced in a rocking-chair. "As Madame Goldmarker says, nobody else in the world would have given her a home these four years, and a good many wouldn't have had her round the house."

"That is true," replied Mary, "and your husband must have been a very good man, from all you tell me, Mrs. Grubb."

"Good enough, but totally uninteresting," said that lady laconically.

"Well, putting aside the question as to whether goodness ought to be totally uninteresting, you say that Lisa's mother left Mr. Grubb three hundred dollars for her food and clothing, and that she has been ever since a willing servant, absolutely devoted to your interests."

"We never put a cent of the three hundred dollars into our own pockets," explained Mrs. Grubb. "Mr. Grubb was dreadfully opposed to my doing it, but every penny of it went to freeing our religious society from debt. It was a case of the greatest good of the greatest number, and I did n't flinch. I thought it was a good deal more important that the Army of Present Perfection should have a roof over its head than that Lisa Bennett should be fed and clothed; that is, if both could not be done."

"I don't know the creed of the Army, but it seems to me your Presently Perfect soldiers would have been rather uncomfortable under their roof, if Lisa Bennett had been naked and starving outside."

"Oh, it would never have come to that," responded Mrs. Grubb easily. "There is plenty of money in the world, and it belongs equally to the whole human race. I don't recognize anybody's right to have a dollar more than I have; but Mr. Grubb could never accept any belief that had been held less than a thousand years, and before he died he gave some money to a friend of his, and told him to pay me ten dollars every month towards Lisa's board. Untold gold could never pay for what my pride has suffered in having her, and if she had n't been so useful I could n't have done it, — I don't pretend that I could. She 's an offense to the eye.''

"Not any longer," said Mary proudly.

"Well, she was, up to a few months ago; but she would always do anything for the twins, and though they are continually getting into mischief, she never lets any harm come to them, not so much as a scratch. If I 'd taken a brighter child, she would have been forever playing on her own account and thinking of her own pleasure; but if you once get an idea into Lisa's head of what you expect her to do, she will go on doing it to the end of the world, and wild horses could n't keep her from it.''

"It 's a pity more of us had n't that virtue of obedience to a higher law.''

"Well, perhaps it is, and perhaps it is n't; it 's a sign of a very weak mind.''

"Or a very strong one," retorted Mary.

"There are natural leaders and natural followers," remarked Mrs. Grubb smilingly, as she swayed to and fro in Mary's rocking-chair. Her smile, like a ballet dancer's, had no connection with, nor relation to, the matter of her speech or her state of feeling; it was what a watchmaker would call a detached movement. "I can't see," said she, "that it is my duty to send Lisa away to be taught, just when I need her most. My development is a good deal more important than hers."

"Why?"

"Why? Because I have a vocation and a mission; because, if I should falter or faint by the wayside, hundreds of women who depend on me for inspiration would fall back into error and suffer permanent loss and injury."

"Do you suppose they really would?" asked Mary rather maliciously, anxious if possible to ruffle the surface of Mrs. Grubb's exasperating placidity. "Or would they, of course after a long period of grief-stricken apathy, attach themselves to somebody else's classes?"

"They might," allowed Mrs. Grubb, in a tone of hurt self-respect, "though you must know, little as you've seen of the world, that no one woman has just the same revelation as any other, and that there are some who are born to interpret truth to the multitude. I can say in all humility that it has been so with me from a child. I 've always had a burning desire to explore the secret chambers of Thought, always yearned to understand and explain the universe."

"I have never tried to explain it," sighed Mary a little wearily; "one is so busy trying to keep one's little corner clean and sweet and pleasant, a helpful place where sad and tired souls can sit down and rest."

"Who wants to sit down and rest? Not I!" exclaimed Mrs. Grubb. "But then, I 'm no criterion, I have such an active mind."

"There are just a few passive virtues," said Mary teasingly. "We must remember that activity does n't always make for good; sometimes it is unrest, disintegration; not growth, Mrs. Grubb, but fermentation."

Mrs. Grubb took out a small blank-book and made a note, for she had an ear for any sentence that might be used in a speech.

"That is true. ' *Distrust the activity which is not growth, but fermentation :* ' that will just hit some ladies in my classes, and it comes right in with something I am going to say this evening. We have a Diet Congress here this week, and there 's a good deal of feeling and dispute between the various branches. I have two delegates stopping with me, and they have n't spoken to each other since yesterday morning, nor sat down to eat at the same table. I shall do all I can, as the presiding officer, to keep things pleasant at the meetings, but it will be difficult. You 've never been in public life and can't understand it, but you see there are women among the delegates who 've suffered the tyranny of man so long that they will cook anything their husbands demand; women who believe in eating any kind of food, and hold that the principal trouble lies in bad cooking; women who will give up meat, but still indulge in all sorts of cakes, pastries, and kickshaws; and women who are strong on temperance in drink, but who see no need of temperance in food. The whole question of diet reform is in an awful state, and a Congress is the only way to settle it."

"How do men stand on the diet question?" asked Mary, with a twinkle in her eye.

"They don't stand at all," answered Mrs. Grubb promptly. "They sit right still, and some of them lie down flat, you might say, whenever it's mentioned. They'll do even more for temperance than they will for reformed diet, though goodness knows they're fond enough of drinking. The Edenites number about sixty-seven in this city, and nine is the largest number of gentlemen that we've been able to interest. Those nine are the husbands and sons of the lady members, and at the next meeting two of them are going to be expelled for backsliding. I declare, if I was a man, I'd be ashamed to confess that I was all stomach; but that's what most of them are. Not that it's easy work to be an Edenite; it's impossible to any but a highly spiritual nature. I have been on the diet for six months, and nothing but my position as vice-president of the society, and my desire to crush the body and release the spirit, could have kept me faithful. I don't pretend to like it, but that does n't make me disloyal. There's nothing I enjoy better than a good cut of underdone beef, with plenty of dish gravy; I love nice tender porterhouse steaks with mushrooms; I love thick mutton-chops broiled over a hot fire: but I can't believe in them, and my conscience won't allow me to eat them. Do you believe in meat?"

"Certainly."

"I don't see why you say ' certainly.' You would be a good deal better off without it. You are filling yourself full of carnal, brutal, murderous passions every time you eat it. The people who eat meat are not half so elevated nor half so teachable as the Edenites."

"The Edenites are possibly too weak and hungry to resist instruction," said Mary.

"They are neither weak nor hungry," replied their vice-president, with dignity. "They eat milk, and stewed fruit, and all the edible grains nicely boiled. It stands to reason that if you can subdue your earthly, devilish, sensual instincts on anything, you can do it on a diet like that. You can't fancy an angel or a Mahatma devouring underdone beef."

"No," agreed Mistress Mary; "but for that matter, the spectacle of an angel eating dried-apple sauce does n't appeal to my imagination."

"It 's no joking matter," said Mrs. Grubb, with real tears in her eyes. "It was my interest in Theosophy that brought me to the Edenic diet. I have good and sufficient motives for denying my appetite, for I've got a certain goal to reach, and I'm in earnest."

"Then here's my hand, and I respect you for it. Oh, how I should like a hot mutton-chop at this moment! — Do forgive me."

"I forgive you, because I can see you act up to all the light that has been revealed to you. I don't know as I ought to be proud because I see so much truth. My classes tell me I get these marvelous revelations because I'm so open-minded. Now Mr. Grubb wouldn't and couldn't bear discussion of any sort. His soul never grew, for he wouldn't open a chink where a new idea might creep in. He'd always accompany me to all my meetings (such advantages as that man had and missed!), and sometimes he'd take the admission tickets; but when the speaking began, he'd shut the door and stay out in the entry by himself till it was time to wait upon me home. Do you believe in vaccination?"

"Certainly."

"Well, it passes my comprehension how you can be so sure of your beliefs. You'd better come and hear some of the arguments on the opposite side. I am the secretary

of the Anti-Vaccination League." (Mrs.
Grubb was especially happy in her anti-
societies; negatives seemed to give her more
scope for argument.) "I say to my classes,
'You must not blame those to whom higher
truths do not appeal, for refusing to believe
in that which they cannot understand; but
you may reprove them for decrying or ridi-
culing those laws or facts of nature which
they have never investigated with an un-
prejudiced mind.' Well, I must be going.
I've sat longer than I meant to, this room
is so peaceful and comfortable."

"But what about Lisa's future? We
have n't settled that, although we've had
a most interesting and illuminating conversation."

"Why, I've told you how I feel about
her, and you must respect my feeling. The
world can only grow when each person
allows his fellow man complete liberty of
thought and action. I've kept the child
four years, and now when my good care
and feeding, together with the regular work
and early hours I've always prescribed,
have begun to show their fruits in her improved condition, you want she should be
put in some institution. Why is n't she

doing well enough as she is? I'm sure
you've had a wonderful influence over her."

"Nothing could induce me to lose sight
of her entirely," said Mistress Mary, "but
we feel now that she is ready to take the
next step. She needs a skilled physician
who is master both of body and mind, as
well as a teacher who is capable of following out his principles. I will see to all
that, if you will only give me the privilege."

Mrs. Grubb sank down in the rocking-
chair in despair. "Don't I need some consideration as well as that little imbecile?
Am I, with my ambitions and aspirations,
to be forever hampered by these three night-
mares of children? Oh, if I could once
get an astral body, I would stay in it, you
may be sure!"

"You do not absolutely need Lisa yourself," argued Mary. "It is the twins to
whom she has been indispensable. Provide
for them in some way, and she is freed from
a responsibility for which she is not and
never was fit. It is a miracle that some
tragedy has not come out of this daily com-
panionship of three such passionate, irresponsible creatures."

"Some tragedy will come out of it yet,"

said Mrs. Grubb gloomily, " if I am not freed from the shackles that keep me in daily slavery. The twins are as likely to go to the gallows as anywhere; and as for Lisa, she would be a good deal better off dead than alive, as Mrs. Sylvester says."

"That isn't for us to decide," said Mistress Mary soberly. "I might have been careless and impertinent enough to say it a year ago, but not now. Lisa has all along been the victim of cruel circumstances. Wherever she has been sinned against through ignorance, it is possible, barely possible, that the fault may be atoned for; but any neglect of duty now would be a criminal offense. It does not behoove us to be too scornful when we remember that the taint (fortunately a slight one) transmitted to poor little Lisa existed in greater or less degree in Handel and Molière, Julius Cæsar, Napoleon, Petrarch, and Mohammed. The world is a good deal richer for them, certainly."

Mrs. Grubb elevated her head, the light of interest dawned in her eye, and she whipped her note-book out of her pocket.

"Is that a fact?" she asked excitedly.

"It is a fact."

"Is it generally known?"

"It must be known by all who have any interest in the education of defective persons, since it touches one of the bugbears which they have to fight."

"Is there any society in this city devoted to the study of such problems?"

"There is a society which is just on the point of opening an institution for the training of defective children."

Mrs. Grubb's face fell, and her hand relaxed its grasp upon the pencil. (If there was anything she enjoyed, it was the sensation of being a pioneer in any movement.) Presently she brightened again.

"If it is just starting," she said, "then it must need more members, and speakers to stir up the community. Now I am calculated, by constant association with a child of this character, to be of signal service to the cause. Not many persons have had my chance to observe phenomena. Just give me a letter to the president, — have they elected officers yet? — where do they meet? — and tell him I 'll call on him and throw all the weight of my influence on his side. It 's wonderful! Handel, Molière, Buddha, was it — Buddha? — Cæsar, Petrarch, and

Wellington, — no, not Wellington. Never mind, I'll get a list from you to-morrow and look it all up, — it's perfectly marvelous! And I have one of this great, unhappy, suffering class in my own family, one who may yet be transformed into an Elizabeth Browning or a Joan of Arc!"

Mistress Mary sighed in her heart. She learned more of Mrs. Grubb with every interview, and she knew that her enthusiasms were as discouraging as her apathies.

"How unlucky that I mentioned Napoleon, Cæsar, and Mohammed!" she thought. "I shall be haunted now by the fear that she will go on a lecturing-tour through the country, and exhibit poor Lisa as an interesting example. Mrs. Grubb's mind is like nothing so much as a crazy-quilt."

VIII.

THE YOUNG MINISTER'S PSYCHOLOGICAL OBSERVATIONS.

MRS. GRUBB'S interest in the education of the defective classes was as short-lived as it was ardent. One interview with the president of the society convinced her that he was not a person to be "helped" according to her understanding of the term. She thought him a self-sufficient gentleman, inflexible in demeanor, and inhospitable to anybody's ideas or anybody's hobbies but his own. She resented his praise of Mistress Mary and Rhoda, and regarded it fulsome flattery when he alluded to their experiment with Marm Lisa as one of the most interesting and valuable in his whole experience; saying that he hardly knew which to admire and venerate the more, the genius of the teachers, or the devotion, courage, and docility of the pupil.

In the summer months Lisa had gone to the country with Mistress Mary and Edith, who were determined never to lose sight of her until the end they sought was actually attained. There, in the verdant freshness of that new world, Lisa experienced a strange exaltation of the senses. Every wooded path unfolded treasures of leaf, bud, blossom, and brier, and of beautiful winged things that crept and rustled among the grasses. There was the ever new surprise of the first wild flowers, the abounding mystery of the bird's note and the brook's song, the daily greeting of bees and butterflies, frogs and fishes, field mice and squirrels; so that the universe, which in the dead past had been dreary and without meaning, suddenly became warm and friendly, and she, the alien, felt a sense of kinship with all created things.

Helen had crossed the continent to imbibe the wisdom of the East, and had brought back stores of knowledge to spend in Lisa's service; but Rhoda's sacrifice was perhaps the most complete, for Mrs. Grubb having at first absolutely refused to part with Lisa, Rhoda had flung herself into the breach and taken the twins to her mother's cottage in the mountains.

She came up the broad steps, on a certain

appointed day in August, leading her charges into Mistress Mary's presence. They were clean, well dressed, and somewhat calm in demeanor.

"You may go into the playground," she said, after the greetings were over; "and remember that there are sharp spikes on the high fence by the pepper-tree."

"Mary," she went on impressively, closing the doors and glancing about the room to see if there were any listeners, "Mary, those children have been with me eight weeks, and I do — not — like — them. What are you going to do with me? Wait, I have n't told you the whole truth, — I *dis*like them actively. As for my mother, she is not committed to any theory about the essential integrity of infancy, and she positively abhors them."

"Then they are no more likable in the bosom of the family than they have been here?" asked Mary, in a tone of disappointment.

"More likable? They are less so! Do you see any change in me, — a sort of spiritual effulgence, a saintly radiance, such as comes after a long spell of persistent virtue? Because there ought to be, if my summer has served its purpose."

"Poor dear rosy little martyr! Sit down and tell me all about it."

"Well, we have kept a log, but " —

" '*We?*' What, Rhoda, did you drag your poor mother into the experiment?"

"Mother? No, she generally locked herself in her room when the twins were indoors, but — well, of course I had help of one sort and another with them. I have held to your plan of discipline pretty well; at any rate, I have n't administered corporal punishment, although if I had whipped them whenever they actually needed it, I should have worn out all the young minister's slippers."

Mary groaned. "Then there was another young minister? It does n't make any difference, Rhoda, whether you spend your summers in the woods or by the sea, in the valleys or on the mountains, there is always a young minister. Have all the old ones perished off the face of the earth, pray? And what do the young ones see in you, you dear unregenerate, that they persist in following you about, threatening my peace of mind and your future career? Well, go on!"

"Debarred from the use of the persuasive

but obsolete slipper," Rhoda continued
evasively, "I tried milder means of discipline, — solitary confinement for one; not
very much, you know, — only seventeen
times in eight weeks. I hope you don't
object to that? Of course it was in a pleasant room with southern exposure, good
view and good ventilation, a thermometer,
picture-books, and all that. It would have
worked better if the twins had n't always
taken the furniture to pieces, and mother is
so fussy about anything of that sort. She
finally suggested the winter bedroom for
Atlantic's incarceration, as it has nothing
in it but a huge coal-stove enveloped in a
somewhat awe-inspiring cotton sheet. I
put in a comfortable low chair, a checker-
board, and some books, fixing the time limit
at half an hour. By the way, Mary, that's
such a pretty idea of yours to leave the door
unlocked, and tell the children to come out
of their own accord whenever they feel at
peace with the community. I tried it, —
oh, I always try your pretty ideas first; but
I had scarcely closed the door before Pacific
was out of it again, a regenerated human
being according to her own account. But
to return to Atlantic. I went to him when

the clock struck, only to discover that he had broken in the circles of isinglass round the body of the coal-stove, removed the ashes with a book, got the dampers out of order, and taken the doors off the hinges! I am sure Mrs. Grubb is right to keep them on bread and milk and apple sauce; a steady diet of beef and mutton would give them a simply unconquerable energy. Oh, laugh as you may, I could never have lived through the ordeal if it had n't been for the young minister!"

"Do you mean that he became interested in the twins?"

"Oh yes! — very deeply interested. You have heard me speak of him: it was Mr. Fielding."

"Why, Rhoda, he was the last summer's minister, the one who preached at the sea-shore."

"Certainly; but he was only supplying a pulpit there; now he has his own parish. He is taking up a course of child-study, and asked me if he was at liberty to use the twins for psychological observations. I assented most gratefully, thinking, you know, that he could n't study them unless he kept them with him a good deal; but he counted without his host, as you can imagine. He lives at the hotel until his cottage is finished, and the first thing I knew he had hired a stout nursemaid as his contribution to the service of humanity. I think he was really sorry for me, for I was so confined I could scarcely ever ride, or drive, or play tennis; and besides, he simply had to have somebody to hold the children while he observed them. We succeeded better after the nurse came, and we all had delightful walks and conversations together, just a nice little family party! The hotel people called Atlantic the Cyclone and Pacific the Warrior. Sometimes strangers took us for the children's parents, and that was embarrassing; not that I mind being mistaken for a parent, but I decline being credited, or discredited, with the maternity of those imps!"

"They are altogether new in my experience," confessed Mary.

"That is just what the young minister said."

"Will he keep up his psychological investigation during the autumn?" Mary inquired.

"He really has no material there."

"What will he do then, — carry it on by correspondence?"

"No, that is always unsatisfactory. I fancy he will come here occasionally: it is the most natural place, and he is especially eager to meet you."

"Of course!" said Mistress Mary, reciting provokingly: —

> "'My lyre I tune, my voice I raise,
>   But with my numbers mix my sighs,
>   And whilst I sing Euphelia's praise
>   I fix my soul on Chloe's eyes.'

How delightful," she added, "how inspiring it is to see a young man so devoted to science, particularly to this neglected science! I shall be charmed to know more of his psychology and observe his observations."

"He is extremely clever."

"I have no doubt of it from what you tell me, both clever and ingenious."

"And his cottage is lovely; it will be finished and furnished by next summer, — Queen Anne, you know."

Now this was so purely irrelevant that there was a wicked hint of intention about it, and though Mistress Mary was smiling (and quaking) in the very depths of her heart, she cruelly led back the conversation into safe educational channels. "Isn't it curious," she said, "that we should have thought Lisa, not the twins, the impossible problem? Yet, as I have written you, her solution is something to which we can look forward with reasonable confidence. It is scarcely eighteen months, but the work accomplished is almost incredible, even to me, and I have watched and counted every step."

"The only explanation must be this," said Rhoda, "that her condition was largely the fruit of neglect and utter lack of comprehension. The state of mind and body in which she came to us was out of all proportion to the moving cause, when we discovered it. Her mother thought she would be an imbecile, the Grubbs treated her as one, and nobody cared to find out what she really was or could be."

"Her brain had been writ upon by the 'moving finger,'" quoted Mary, "though the writing was not graved so deep but that love and science could erase it. You remember the four lines in Omar Khayyàm?

"'The moving finger writes; and, having writ,
　Moves on: nor all your piety nor wit
　　Shall lure it back to cancel half a line,
　Nor all your tears wash out a word of it.'"

"Edith says I will hardly know her," said Rhoda.

"It is true. The new physician is a genius, and physically and outwardly she has changed more in the last three months than in the preceding year. She 'dresses herself neatly now, braids her own hair, and ties her ribbons prettily. Edith has kept up her gymnastics, and even taught her to row and play nine-pins. For the first time in my life, Rhoda, I can fully understand a mother's passion for a crippled, or a blind, or a defective child. I suppose it was only Lisa's desperate need that drew us to her at first. We all loved and pitied her, even at the very height of her affliction; but now she fascinates me. I know no greater pleasure than the daily miracle of her growth. She is to me the sister I never had, the child I never shall have. When we think of our success with this experiment, we must try to keep our faith in human nature, even under the trying ordeal of the twins."

"My faith in human nature is absolutely intact," answered Rhoda; "the trouble is that the Warrior and the Cyclone are not altogether human. Atlantic is the cold-

est creature I ever knew, — so cold that
he could stand the Shadrach-Meshech-and-
Abednego test with impunity; Pacific is
hot, — so hot-tempered that one can hardly
touch her without being scorched. If I
had money enough to conduct an expensive
experiment, I would separate them, and
educate Pacific at the North Pole and
Atlantic in the tropics."

"If they are not distinctly human, we
must allow them a few human virtues at
least," said Mary; "for example, their loyalty to each other. Pacific, always at war
with the community, seldom hurts her brother; Atlantic, selfish and grasping with
all the world, shares generously with his
sister. We must remember, too, that Lisa's
care has been worse than nothing for them,
notwithstanding its absolute fidelity, and
their dependence has been a positive injury
to her. There! she has just come into
the playground with Edith. Will wonders
never cease? Pacific is embracing her
knees, and Atlantic allows himself to be
hugged!"

Marm Lisa was indeed beside herself
with joy at the meeting. She clung to the
infant rebels, stroked their hair, admired

their aprons, their clean hands, their new
boots; and, on being smartly slapped by
Atlantic for putting the elastic of his hat
behind his ears, kissed his hand as if it had
offered a caress. "He's so little," she said
apologetically, looking up with wet eyes to
Edith, who stood near.

IX.

MARM LISA'S QUEST.

IT was not long after this conversation that the twins awoke one morning with a very frenzy of adventure upon them. It was accompanied by a violent reaction against all the laws of God and man, and a desire to devour the tree of knowledge, fruit, limbs, and trunk, no matter at what cost.

We have no means of knowing whether there was an excess of electricity in the atmosphere, whether their youthful livers were disordered, or whether the Evil One was personally conducting the day's exercises; judged by the light of subsequent events, all of these suppositions might easily have been true. During the morning they so demeaned themselves that all Mistress Mary's younger neophytes became apostates to the true faith, and went over in a body to the theory of the total depravity of unbaptized infants.

In the afternoon they did not appear, nor did Marm Lisa. This was something that had never occurred before, save when Pacific had a certain memorable attack of mumps that would have carried off any child who was fitted for a better world, or one who was especially beloved.

"Do you suppose anything is wrong?" asked Mary nervously.

"Of course not," said Edith. "I remember seeing Lisa in the playground at one o'clock, but my impression is that she was alone, and stayed only a moment. At any rate, I was very busy and did not speak to her. Mrs. Grubb has probably taken the twins to have their hair cut, or something of that sort."

"What a ridiculous suggestion!" exclaimed Rhoda. "You know perfectly well that Mrs. Grubb would never think of cutting their hair, if it swept the earth! She may possibly have taken them to join a band; they must be getting to a proper age for membership. At any rate, I will call there and inquire, on my way home, although I can never talk to Mrs. Grubb two minutes without wanting to shake her."

Rhoda made her promised visit, but the

house was closed, and the neighbors knew
nothing of the whereabouts of the children
beyond the fact that Mrs. Grubb was seen
talking to them as she went into the yard,
a little after twelve o'clock. Rhoda naturally concluded, therefore, that Edith's
supposition must be correct, and that Mrs.
Grubb had for once indulged in a family
excursion.

Such was not the case, however. After
luncheon, Marm Lisa had washed the twins'
hands and faces in the back yard as usual,
and left them for an instant to get a towel
from the kitchen. When she returned, she
looked blankly about, for there was no sign
of the two dripping faces and the uplifted
streaming hands. They had a playful habit
of hiding from her, knowing that in no
other way could they make her so unhappy;
so she stood still for some moments, calling
them, at first sharply, then piteously, but
with no result. She ran to the front gate:
it was closed; the rope-fastening was out of
reach, and plainly too complicated even for
their preternatural powers. She hurried
back to the house, and searched every room
in a bewildered sort of fashion, finding
nothing. As she came out again, her eye

caught sight of a kitchen chair in the corner of the yard. They had climbed the picket fence, then. Yes; Atlantic, while availing himself of its unassuming aid, had left a clue in a fragment of his trousers. She opened the gate, and ran breathlessly along the streets to that Garden of Eden where joy had always hitherto awaited her. Some instinct of fear or secrecy led her to go quietly through all the rooms and search the playground, without telling any one of her trouble. That accomplished fruitlessly, she fled home again, in the vain hope of finding the children in some accustomed haunt overlooked in her first search. She began to be thoroughly alarmed now, and thoroughly confused. With twitching hands and nervous shaking of the head, she hurried through the vacant rooms, growing more and more aimless in her quest. She climbed on a tall bureau and looked in a tiny medicine cupboard; then under the benches and behind the charts in the parlor; even under the kitchen sink, among the pots and pans, and in the stove, where she poked tremulously in the ashes. Her new-found wit seemed temporarily to have deserted her, and she was a pitiable thing as she wandered about, her breath coming in long-drawn sighs, with now and then a half-stifled sob.

Suddenly she darted into the street again. Perhaps they had followed their aunt Cora. Distance had no place in her terror-stricken heart. She traversed block after block, street after street, until she reached Pocahontas Hall, a building and locality she knew well. She crept softly up the main stairs, and from the landing, slipped into the gallery above. Mrs. Grubb sat in the centre of the stage, with a glass of water, a bouquet of roses, and a bundle of papers and tracts on the table by her side. In the audience were twenty or thirty women and a dozen men, their laps filled, and their pockets bulging, with propaganda. They stood at intervals to ask superfluous or unanswerable questions, upon which Mrs. Grubb would rise and reply, with cheeks growing pink and pinker, with pleasant smile and gracious manner, and a voice fairly surcharged with conviction. Most of the ladies took notes, and a girl with a receding chin was seated at a small table in front of the platform, making a stenographic report.

All this Marm Lisa saw, but her eyes rested on nothing she longed to see. Mrs. Grubb's lecture-voice rose and fell melodiously, floating up to her balcony heights in a kind of echo that held the tone, but not the words. The voice made her drowsy, for she was already worn out with emotion, but she roused herself with an effort, and stole down the stairs to wander into the street again. Ah, there was an idea! The coat-shop! Why had she not thought of it before?

The coat-shop was a sort of clothing manufactory on a small scale, a tall, narrow building four stories high, where she had often gone with Atlantic and Pacific. There were sewing-machines on the ground floor, the cutters and pressers worked in the middle stories, and at the top were the finishers. It was neither an extensive nor an exciting establishment, and its only fascination lay in the fact that the workwomen screamed with laughter at the twins' conversation, and after leading them to their utmost length, teasing and goading them into a towering passion, would stuff them with nuts or dates or cheap sweetmeats. The coat-shop was two or three miles from the hall, and it was closing-time and quite dark when Lisa arrived. She came out of the door after having looked vainly in every room, and sat down dejectedly in the entrance, with her weary head leaning against the wall. There was but a moment's respite for her, for the manager came out of his office, and stumbling over her in the dusk, took her by the shoulders and pushed her into the street with an oath.

"Go and sit on your own doorstep, can't you," he muttered, "and not make me break my legs over you!"

She was too spent to run any farther. She dragged her heavy feet along slowly, almost unconsciously, neither knowing nor caring whither they led her. Home she could not, dared not go, bearing that heavy burden of remorse! Mrs. Grubb would ask for Atlantic and Pacific, and then what would become of her? Mr. Grubb would want to give Pacific her milk. No, Mr. Grubb was dead. There! she had n't looked in the perambulator. No, there was n't any perambulator. That was dead, too, and gone away with Mr. Grubb. There used to be babies, two babies, in the perambulator. What had become of them?

Were they lost, too? And the umbrella
that she used to hold until her arm ached,
and the poor pale weeping mother always
lying on a bed, — were they all gone together? Her head buzzed with worrying, un-
related thoughts, so that she put up her
hands and held it in place on her shoulders
as she shuffled wearily along. A heavy
dripping mist began to gather and fall, and
she shivered in the dampness, huddling herself together and leaning against the houses
for a shelter. She sat down on the curbstone and tried to think, staring haggardly
at the sign on the corner fruit-shop. In
that moment she suddenly forgot the reason
of her search. She had lost — what? She
could not go home to Eden Place, but why?
Oh yes! it came to her now: there was
something about a perambulator, but it all
seemed vague to her. Suddenly a lamp-
lighter put his ladder against a post in front
of her, and climbing up nimbly lighted the
gas-jet inside of the glass frame. It shone
full on a flight of broad steps, a picture so
much a part of her life-dream that she
would go up to the very gate of heaven with
its lines burned into her heart and brain.

She crept up and turned the knob of the

outer door. It was unlocked, and she stole into the inner room, the Paradise, place of joy and sweet content, heart's rest, soul's heaven, love's own abode. The very atmosphere soothed her. She heard the janitress clatter through the halls, lock the door, and descend the stairs to her own rooms in the basement. The light from the street lamps shone in at the two end windows, so that the room was not in utter darkness. She would lie down here and die with Mr. Grubb and the babies and the umbrella. Atlantic and Pacific would be sure to come back; nobody who had ever known it could live without this place. Miss Mary would find them. She would make everything right. The mere thought of Mistress Mary brought a strange peace into poor Lisa's overwrought, distraught mind.

She opened the closet door. It was as dainty and neat as Mistress Mary herself, and the mere sight of it bred order in Lisa's thoughts. On the top of a pile of envelopes lay the sewing-picture that Atlantic had spoiled that day. It had been a black morning, and the bit of cardboard was torn and soiled and bent. Lisa looked at it with a maternal and a prophetic eye. She could

see the firm line of Rhoda's lip as she bore
down upon the destructive urchin. She
could almost hear the bright challenging
tone as Rhoda would say: "Now, Atlantic,
let us see what we can do! Cut off the
chewed edges with these scissors, paste these
thin pieces of paper over the torn places,
and rub the card with this crust of bread.
A new one? Certainly *not*, my young
friend!"

Lisa took the poor little object in her
hand, and seeing Mistress Mary's white
apron, pressed her cheek against it in a
transport of tenderness and hung it over
her arm. Just then she caught sight of the
clay bird's-nest that Pacific had modeled,
— such a lovely bird's-nest that it had been
kept for the cabinet. She carried her treasures over to the old-fashioned lounge where
the babies took their occasional nap, put
them carefully in a small red chair close
beside it, and then, stretching her weary
length on the cushions, she kissed the
smooth folds of the apron and clasped it in
her arms.

Mistress Mary would come soon. She
would come in her cloud of white, and her
steel fillet would gleam and shine when the

sunshine fell upon it, and make star-rays and moonbeams and lightning-flashes; and the tiny points would twinkle and wink and laugh and blink whenever she turned her head. She would smile, and everything would suddenly be clear; she would speak, and the weary buzzing of windmills in the brain would be hushed. Under her touch the darkness and heaviness would vanish, and there would be no more night there, — no more night.

As these healing visions stole upon Marm Lisa, the torture and the anguish, the long hours of bewilderment, faded little by little, little by little, till at length a blessed sleep crept over her eyelids, blotting into a merciful nothingness the terror and the misery of the day.

X.

THE TWINS JOIN THE CELESTIALS.

MEANWHILE, Atlantic and Pacific had been enjoying themselves even unto the verge of delirium. In the course of their wanderings they had come upon a Chinaman bearing aloft a huge red silken banner crowned by a badger's tail. Everything young that had two legs was following him, and they joined the noble army of followers. As they went on, other Chinamen with other banners came from the side-alleys, and all at once the small procession thus formed turned a corner and came upon the parent body, a sight that fairly stunned them by its Oriental magnificence. It was the four thousandth anniversary of the birth of Yeong Wo, had the children realized it (and that may have been the reason that they awoke in a fever of excitement), — Yeong Wo, statesman, philanthropist, philosopher, and poet; and the great day had been chosen to dedicate the new temple and

install in it a new joss, and to exhibit a
monster dragon just arrived from China.
The joss had been sitting in solemn state in
his sanctum sanctorum for a week, while
the priests appeased him hourly with plen-
teous libations of rice brandy, sacrifices of
snow-white pigeons, and offerings of var-
nished pork. Clouds of incense had regaled
his expansive mahogany nostrils, while his
ears of ivory inlaid with gold and bronze
had been stimulated with the ceaseless clashing of gongs and wailings of Chinese fiddles.
Such homage and such worship would have
touched a heart of stone, and that of the
joss was penetrable sandalwood; so as the
days of preparation wore away, the smile
on the teakwood lips of the idol certainly
became more propitious. This was greatly
to the satisfaction of the augurs and the
high priest; for a mighty joss is not always
in a sunny humor on feast-days, and to
parade a sulky god through the streets is a
very depressing ceremony, foretelling to the
initiated a season of dire misfortune. So
his godship smiled and shook his plume of
peacock feathers benignantly on Yeong
Wo's birthday, and therefore the pageant
in which Atlantic and Pacific bore a part

was more gorgeous than anything that ever took place out of the Flowery Kingdom itself.

Fortune smiled upon the naughty creatures at the very outset, for Pacific picked up a stick of candy in the street, and gave half of it to a pretty Chinese maiden whose name in English would have been Spring Blossom, and who looked, in any language, like a tropical flower, in her gown of blue-and-gold-embroidered satin and the sheaf of tiny fans in her glossy black hair. Spring Blossom accepted the gift with enthusiasm, since a sweet tooth is not a matter of nationality, and ran immediately to tell her mother, a childish instinct also of universal distribution. She climbed, as nimbly as her queer little shoes would permit, a flight of narrow steps leading to a balcony; while the twins followed close at her heels, and wedged their way through a forest of Mongolian legs till they reached the front, where they peeped through the spaces of the railings with Spring Blossom, Fairy Foot, Dewy Rose, and other Celestial babies, quite overlooked in the crowd and excitement and jollity. Such a very riot of confusion there was, it seemed as if Confucius might have originally spelled his name with an *s* in the middle; for every window was black with pigtailed highbinders, cobblers, pork butchers, and pawnbrokers. The narrow streets and alleys became one seething mass of Asiatic humanity, while the painted belles came out on their balconies like butterflies, sitting among a wealth of gaudy paper flowers that looked pale in comparison with the daubs of vermilion on their cheeks and the rainbow colors of their silken tunics.

At last the pageant had gathered itself together, and came into full view in all its magnificence. There were pagodas in teakwood inlaid with gold and resting on ebony poles, and behind them, on a very tame Rosinante decked with leopard skins and gold bullion fringes, a Chinese maiden dressed to represent a queen of Celestial mythology. Then came more pagodas, and companies of standard-bearers in lavender tunics, red sashes, green and orange leggings and slippers; more and more splendid banners, painted with dragons sprawling in distressed attitudes; litters containing minor gods and the paraphernalia they were accustomed to need on a journey like this; more litters bearing Chinese orchestras, gongs going at full blast, fiddles squeaking, drums rumbling, trumpets shrieking, cymbals clashing, — just the sort of Babel that the twins adored.

And now came the chariot and throne of the great joss himself, and just behind him a riderless bay horse, intended for his imperial convenience should he tire of being swayed about on the shoulders of his twelve bearers, and elect to change his method of conveyance. Behind this honored steed came a mammoth rock-cod in a pagoda of his own, and then, heralded by a fusillade of fire-crackers, the new dragon itself, stretching and wriggling its monster length through one entire block. A swarm of men cleared the way for it, gesticulating like madmen in their zeal to get swimming-room for the sacred monster. Never before in her brief existence had Pacific Simonson been afraid of anything, but if she had been in the street, and had so much as caught the wink of the dragon's eye or a wave of its consecrated fin, she would have dropped senseless to the earth; as it was, she turned her back to the procession, and, embracing with terror-stricken fervor the legs of the

Chinaman standing behind her, made up her mind to be a better girl in the future. The monster was borne by seventy-four coolies who furnished legs for each of the seventy-four joints of its body, while another concealed in its head tossed it wildly about. Little pigtailed boys shrieked as they looked at its gaping mouth that would have shamed a man-eating shark, at the huge locomotive headlights that served for its various sets of eyes, at the horns made of barber poles, and the moustache of twisted hogshead hoops. Behind this baleful creature, came other smaller ones and more flags, and litters with sacrificial offerings, and more musicians, till all disappeared in the distance, and the crowd surged in the direction of the temple.

There was no such good fortune for the twins as an entrance into this holy of holies, for it held comparatively few beside the dignitaries, aristocrats, and wealthy merchants of the colony; but there was still ample material for entertainment, and they paid no heed to the going down of the sun. Why should they, indeed, when there were fascinating opium dens standing hospitably open, where they could have the excitement of entrance even if it were followed by immediate ejectment? As it grew darker, the scene grew more weird and fairy-like, for the scarlet, orange, and blue lanterns began to gleam one by one in the narrow doorways, and from the shadowy corners of the rooms behind them. In every shop were tables laden with Chinese delicacies, — fish, flesh, fowl, tea, rice, whiskey, lichee nuts, preserved limes, ginger, and other sweetmeats; all of which, when not proffered, could be easily purloined, for there was no spirit of parsimony or hostility afloat in the air. In cubby-holes back of the counters, behind the stoves, wherever they could find room for a table, groups of moon-eyed men began to congregate for their nightly game of fan-tan, some of the players and onlookers smoking, while others chewed lengths of peeled sugar-cane.

In the midst of festivities like these the twins would have gone on from bliss to bliss without consciousness of time or place, had not hunger suddenly descended upon them and sleep begun to tug at their eyelids, changing in a trice their joy into sorrow, and their mirth into mourning. Not that they were troubled with any doubts, fears,

or perplexities. True, they had wandered
away from Eden Place, and had not the
slightest idea of their whereabouts. If they
had been a couple of babes in a wood, or
any two respectable lost children of romance,
memories of lullabies and prayers at mother's knee would have precipitated them
at this juncture into floods of tears; but
home to them was simply supper and bed.
The situation did not seem complex to their
minds; the only plan was of course to howl,
and to do it thoroughly, — stand in a corner
of the market-place, and howl in such a
manner that there could be no mistake as
to the significance of the proceeding; when
the crowd collected, — for naturally a crowd
would collect, — simply demand supper and
bed, no matter what supper nor which bed;
eat the first, lie down in the second, and
there you are! If the twins had been older
and more experienced, they would have
known that people occasionally do demand
the necessities of life without receiving
them; but in that case they would also have
known that such a misfortune would never
fall upon a couple of lost children who con-
fide their woes to the public. There was
no preconcerted plan between them, no sys-

tem. They acted without invention, premonition, or reflection. It was their habit to scream, while holding the breath as long as possible, whenever the universe was unfriendly, and particularly when Nature asserted herself in any way; it was a curious fact that they resented the intervention of Nature and Providence with just as much energy as they did the discipline of their care-takers. They screamed now, the moment that the entertainment palled and they could not keep their eyes open without effort, and never had they been more successful in holding their breath and growing black in the face; indeed, Pacific, in the midst of her performance, said to Atlantic, "Yours is purple, how is mine?"

A crowd did gather, inevitably, for the twins' lungs were capable of a body of tone more piercing than that of a Chinese orchestra, and the wonder is that poor Lisa did not hear them as she sat shivering on the curbstone, miles away; for it was her name with which they conjured.

The populace amused itself for a short space of time, watching the fine but misdirected zeal of the performance, and supposing that the parents of the chanting cherubs were within easy reach. It be-

came unpleasant after a while, however, and
a policeman, inquiring into the matter,
marched the two dirty, weary little protest-
ants off to a station near by, — a march
nearly as difficult and bloody as Sherman's
memorable "march to the sea;" for the
children associated nothing so pleasant as
supper and bed with a blue-coated, brass-
buttoned person, and resisted his well-meant
advances with might and main, and tooth
and nail.

The policeman was at last obliged to con-
fine himself to Atlantic, and called a bro-
ther-in-arms to take charge of Pacific. He
was a man who had achieved distinction in
putting down railroad riots, so he was well
calculated for the task, although he was
somewhat embarrassed by the laughter of
the bystanders when his comrade called out
to him, "Take your club, Mike, but don't
use firearms unless your life's in danger!"

The station reached, the usual examination took place. Atlantic never could tell
the name of the street in which he lived,
nor the number of the house. Pacific could,
perhaps, but would not; and it must be
said, in apology for her abnormal defiance,
that her mental operations were somewhat
confused, owing to copious indulgence in

strong tea, ginger, sugar-cane, and dried fish. She had not been wisely approached in the first place, and she was in her sulkiest and most combative humor; in fact, when too urgently pressed for information as to her age, ancestry, and abiding-place, she told the worthy police officer to go to a locality for which he felt utterly unsuited, after a life spent in the exaltation of virtue and the suppression of vice. (The vocabulary of the twins was somewhat poverty-stricken in respect to the polite phrases of society, but in profanity it would have been rich for a parrot or a pirate.) The waifs were presently given into the care of the police matron, and her advice, sought later, was to the effect that the children had better be fed and put to bed, and as little trouble expended upon them as was consistent with a Christian city government.

"It is possible their parents may call for them in the morning," she said acidly, "but I think it is more than likely that they have been deserted. I know if they belonged to me they 'd be lost forever before I tried to find them!" and she rubbed a black-and-blue spot on her person, which, if exposed, would have betrayed the shape, size, and general ground-plan of Pacific's boot.

XI.

RHODA FREES HER MIND.

MORNING dawned, and Mistress Mary and Rhoda went up the flight of broad steps rather earlier than usual, — so early that the janitress, who had been awake half the night with an ailing baby, was just going in to dust the rooms.

It was she who first caught sight of the old sofa and its occupant, and her exclamation drew Mary and Rhoda to the spot. There lay poor Marm Lisa in the dead sleep of exhaustion, her dress torn and wrinkled, her shoes travel-stained, her hair tangled and matted. Their first idea was that the dreaded foe might have descended upon her, and that she had had some terrible seizure with no one near to aid and relieve her. But the longer they looked, the less they feared this; her face, though white and tear-stained, was tranquil, her lips only slightly pale, and her breathing calm and steady. Mary finally noted the pathetic grouping of little objects in the red chair, and, touched by this, began to apprehend the significance of her own white apron close clasped in the child's loyal arms, and fell a-weeping softly on Rhoda's shoulder. "She needed me, Rhoda," she said. "I do not know for what, but I am sure she needed me."

"I see it all," said Rhoda, administering soft strokes of consolation: "it is something to do with those little beasts; yes, I will call them beasts, and if you don't let me, I 'll call them brutes. They lost themselves yesterday, of course, and dear old Lisa searched for them all the afternoon and half the night, for aught we know, and then came here to be comforted, I suppose, — the blessed thing!"

"Hush! don't touch her," Mary whispered, as Rhoda went impetuously down on her knees by the sofa; "and we must not talk in this room, for fear of waking her. Suppose you go at once to Mrs. Grubb's, dear, and whatever you learn about the twins there, I shall meanwhile call a carriage and take Lisa home to my own bed. The janitress can send Edith to me as soon as she comes, and I will leave her with Lisa while I run back here to consult with

you and Helen. I shall telegraph for Dr.
Thorne, also, to be sure that this sleep is as
natural and healing a thing as it appears to
be."

Mrs. Grubb was surprised, even amused,
at Rhoda's exciting piece of news, but she
was perfectly tranquil.

"Well, don't they beat all!" she exclaimed, leaning against the door-frame
and taking her side hair out of waving-pins
as she talked. "No, I have n't seen them
since noon yesterday. I was out to a picnic
supper at the Army Headquarters at night,
and did n't get home till later than usual,
so I did n't go up to their room. I thought
they were in bed; they always have been in
bed when it was bedtime, ever since they
were born." Here she removed the last
pin, and put it with the others in the bosom
of her dress for safe-keeping. "This morning, when they did n't turn up, I thought
some of you girls had taken a fancy to keep
them over night; I did n't worry, supposing
that Lisa was with them."

"Nobody on earth could take a fancy to
the twins or keep them an hour longer than
necessary, and you know it, Mrs. Grubb,"
said Rhoda, who seldom minced matters;

"and in case no one should ever have the bad manners to tell you the whole truth, I want to say here and now that you neglect everything good and sensible and practical, — all the plain simple duties that stare you directly in the face, — and waste yourself on matters that are of no earthly use to anybody. Those children would have been missed last night if you had one drop of mother's blood in your veins! You have three helpless children under what you are pleased to call your care " (and here Rhoda's lip curled so scornfully that Mrs. Grubb was tempted to stab her with a curling-pin), "and you went to sleep without knowing to a certainty whether they had had supper or bed! I don't believe you are a woman at all, — you are just a vague abstraction; and the only things you 've ever borne or nursed or brooded in your life have been your miserable bloodless little clubs and bands and unions!"

Rhoda's eyes flashed summer lightning, her nostrils quivered, her cheeks flamed scarlet, and Mrs. Grubb sat down suddenly and heavily on the front stairs and gasped for breath. According to her own belief, her whole life had been passed in a search for truth, but it is safe to say she had never before met it in so uncompromising and disagreeable a shape.

"Perhaps when you are quite through with your billingsgate," she finally said, "you will take yourself off my steps before you are ejected. You! to presume to criticise me! You, that are so low in the scale of being, you can no more understand my feelings and motives than a jellyfish can comprehend a star! Go back and tell Miss Mary," she went on majestically, as she gained confidence and breath, "that it is her duty and business to find the children, since they were last seen with her, and unless she proves more trustworthy they will not be allowed to return to her. Tell her, too, that when she wishes to communicate with me, she must choose some other messenger besides you, you impudent, groveling little earthworm! Get out of my sight, or you will unfit me for my classes!"

Mrs. Grubb was fairly superb as she launched these thunderbolts of invective; the staircase her rostrum, her left hand poised impressively on the baluster, and the three snaky strands of brown hair that had writhed out of the waving-pins hissing Medusa-wise on each side of her head.

Rhoda was considerably taken aback by the sudden and violent slamming of the door of number one, Eden Place, and she felt an unwelcome misgiving as to her wisdom in bringing Mrs. Grubb face to face with truth. Her rage had somewhat subsided by the time she reached Mistress Mary's side, for she had stopped on the way to ask a policeman to telephone the various stations for news of the lost children, and report at once to her. "There is one good thing," she thought: "wherever they may be, their light cannot be hid any more than that of a city that is set on a hill. There will be plenty of traces of their journey, for once seen they are never forgotten. Nobody but a hero would think of kidnapping them, and nobody but an idiot would expect a ransom for them!"

"I hope you did n't upbraid Mrs. Grubb," said Mary, divining from Rhoda's clouded brow that her interview had not been a pleasant one. "You know our only peaceful way of rescuing Lisa from her hold is to make a friend of her, and convert her to our way of thinking. Was she much disturbed about the children?"

"Disturbed!" sniffed Rhoda, disdainfully. "Imagine Mrs. Grubb disturbed about anything so trivial as a lost child! If it had been a lost amendment, she might have been ruffled!"

"What is she doing about it, and in what direction is she searching?"

"She is doing nothing, and she will do nothing; she has gone to a Theosophy lecture, and we are to find the twins; and she says it's your fault, anyway, and unless you prove more trustworthy the seraphs will be removed from your care; and you are not to send me again as a messenger, if you please, because I am an impudent, groveling little earth-worm!"

"Rhoda!"

"Yes'm!"

"Did she call you that?"

"Yes'm, and a jellyfish besides; in fact, she dragged me through the entire animal kingdom; but she is a stellar being, — she said so."

"What did you say to her to provoke that, Rhoda? She is thoroughly illogical and perverse, but she is very amiable."

"Yes, when you don't interfere with her. You should catch her with her hair in waving-pins, just after she has imbibed apple sauce! Oh, I can't remember exactly what I said, for I confess I was a trifle heated, and at the moment I thought only of freeing my mind. Let me see: I told her she neglected all the practical duties that stared her directly in the face, and squandered herself on useless fads and vagaries, — that's about all. No-o, now that I come to think of it, I did say that the children would have been missed and found last night, if she had had a drop of mother's blood in her veins.

"That's terse and strong — and tactful," said Mary; "anything more?"

"No, I don't think so. Oh yes! now that I reflect, I said I didn't believe she was a woman at all. That seemed to enrage her beyond anything, somehow; and when I explained it, and tried to modify it by saying I meant that she had never borne or loved or brooded anything in her life but her nasty little clubs, she was white with anger, and told me I was too low in the scale of being to understand her. Good gracious! I wish she understood herself half as well as I understand her!"

Mary gave a hysterical laugh. "I can't pretend you didn't speak the truth, Rhoda, but I am sadly afraid it was ill advised to wound Mrs. Grubb's vanity. Do you feel a good deal better?"

"No," confessed Rhoda penitently. "I did for fifteen minutes, — yes, nearly half an hour; but now I feel worse than ever."

"That is one of the commonest symptoms of freeing one's mind," observed Mary quietly.

It was scarcely an hour later when Atlantic and Pacific were brought in by an officer, very dirty and disheveled, but gay and irresponsible as larks, nonchalant, amiable, and unrepentant. As Rhoda had prophesied, there had been no difficulty in finding them; and as everybody had prophesied, once found there had not been a second's delay in delivery. Moved by fiery hatred of the police matron, who had illustrated justice more than mercy, and illustrated it with the back of a hair-brush on their reversed persons; lured also by two popcorn balls, a jumping-jack, and a tin horse, they accepted the municipal escort with alacrity; and nothing was ever jauntier than the manner in which Pacific, all smiles and molasses, held up her sticky lips for an expected salute, — an unusual offer which was respectfully declined as a matter of discipline.

Mary longed for Rhoda's young minister in the next half-hour, which she devoted to private spiritual instruction. Psychology proved wholly unequal to the task of fathoming the twins, and she fancied that theology might have been more helpful. Their idea seemed to be — if the rudimentary thing she unearthed from their consciousness could be called an idea — that they would not mind repenting if they could see anything of which to repent. Of sin, as sin, they had no apparent knowledge, either by sight, by hearsay, or by actual acquaintance. They sat stolidly in their little chairs, eyes roving to the windows, the blackboard, the pictures; they clubbed together and fished a pin from a crack in the floor during one of Mary's most thrilling appeals; finally, they appeared so bored by the whole proceeding that she felt a certain sense of embarrassment in the midst of her despair. She took them home herself at noon, apologized to the injured Mrs. Grubb for Rhoda's unfortunate remarks, and told that lady, gently but firmly, that Lisa could not be moved until she was decidedly better.

"She was wandering about the streets searching for the twins from noon till long after dark, Mrs. Grubb, — there can be no doubt of it; and she bears unmistakable signs of having suffered deeply. I have called in a physician, and we must all abide by his advice."

"That's well enough for the present," agreed Mrs. Grubb reluctantly, "but I cannot continue to have my studies broken in upon by these excitements. I really cannot. I thought I had made an arrangement with Madame Goldmarker to relieve me, but she has just served me a most unladylike and deceitful trick, and the outcome of it will be that I shall have to send Lisa to the asylum. I can get her examined by the commissioners some time before Christmas, and if they decide she's imbecile they'll take her off my hands. I didn't want to part with her till the twins got older, but I've just found a possible home for them if I can endure their actions until New Year's. Our Army of Present Perfection isn't progressing as it ought to, and it's going to found a colony down in San Diego County, and advertise for children to bring up in the faith. A certain number of men and women have agreed to go and start the thing, and I'm sure my sister, if she was

alive, would be glad to donate her children
to such a splendid enterprise. If the commissioners won't take Lisa, she can go to
Soul Haven, too, — that's the name of the
place;—but no, of course they would n't want
any but bright children, that would grow
up and spread the light." (Mary smiled at
the thought of the twins engaged in the
occupation of spreading light.) "I shall
not join the community myself, though I
believe it's a good thing; but a very different future is unveiling itself before me"
(her tone was full of mystery here), "and
some time, if I can ever pursue my inves-
tigations in peace, you will knock at this
door and I shall have vanished! But I
shall know of your visit, and the very sound
of your footfall will reach my ear, even if
I am inhabiting some remote mountain fast-
ness!"

When Lisa awoke that night, she heard
the crackling of a wood fire on the hearth;
she felt the touch of soft linen under her
aching body, and the pressure of something
cool and fragrant on her forehead. Her
right hand, feebly groping the white counterpane, felt a flower in its grasp. Opening

her eyes, she saw the firelight dancing on tinted walls, and an angel of deliverance sitting by her bedside, — a dear familiar woman angel, whose fair crowned head rose from a cloud of white, and whose sweet downward gaze held all of benignant mother-hood that God could put into woman's eyes.

Marm Lisa looked up dumbly and won-deringly at first, but the mind stirred, thought flowed in upon it, a wave of pain broke over her heart, and she remembered all; for remembrance, alas, is the price of reason.

"Lost! my twinnies, all lost and gone!" she whispered brokenly, with long, shudder-ing sobs between the words. "I look — look — look; never, never find!"

"No, no, dear," Mary answered, stroking the lines from her forehead, "not lost any more; found, Lisa, — do you understand? They are found, they are safe and well, and nobody blames you; and you are safe, too, your new self, your best self unharmed, thank God; so go to sleep, little sister, and dream happy dreams!"

Glad tears rushed from the poor child's eyes, tears of conscious happiness, and the burden rolled away from her heart now, as

yesterday's whirring shuttles in her brain
had been hushed into silence by her long
sleep. She raised her swimming eyes to
Mistress Mary's with a look of unspeakable
trust. "I love you! oh, I love, love, love
you!" she whispered, and, holding the flower
close to her breast, she breathed a sigh of
sweet content, and sank again into quiet
slumber.

XII.

FLOTSAM AND JETSAM.

It may be said in justice to Mrs. Grubb that she was more than usually harassed just at this time.

Mrs. Sylvester, her voluble next-door neighbor, who had lifted many sordid cares from her shoulders, had suddenly become tired of the "new method of mental healing," and during a brief absence of Mrs. Grubb from the city had issued a thousand embossed gilt-edged cards, announcing herself as a Hand Reader in the following terms : —

TO THE ELITE LADIES AND GENTLEMEN OF THE CITY !

I take this method of introducing myself to your kind consideration as a Hand Reader of *rare* and *genuine merit ;* catering merely to the Creme du le Creme of this city. No others need apply.

Having been educated carefully and refinedly, speaking French fluently, therefore I only wish to deal with the elite of the bon-ton.

I do not advertise in papers nor at residence.
Ladies $1.50.   Gents $2.
            Yours truly,
                MRS. PANSY SYLVESTER,
                    3 Eden Place near 4th,
                            Lower bell.
P. S. Pupil of S. CORA GRUBB.

Inasmuch as Mrs. Sylvester had imbibed
all her knowledge from Mrs. Grubb, that
prophet and scholar thought, not unnatu-
rally, that she might have been consulted
about the enterprise, particularly as the
cards were of a nature to prejudice the better class of patients, and lower the social
tone of the temple of healing.

As if this were not vexatious enough, her
plans were disarranged in another and more
important particular. Mrs. Sylvester's manicure had set up a small establishment
for herself, and admitted as partner a certain chiropodist named Boone. The two
artists felt that by sharing expenses they
might increase profits, and there was a
sleeping thought in both their minds that
the partnership might ripen into marriage
if the financial returns of the business were
satisfactory. It was destined, however, to
be a failure in both respects; for Dr. Boone

looked upon Madame Goldmarker, the vocal teacher in number thirteen, Eden Place, and to look upon her was to love her madly, since she earned seventy-five dollars a month, while the little manicure could barely eke out a slender and uncertain twenty. In such crises the heart can be trusted to leap in the right direction and beat at the proper rate.

Mrs. Grubb would have had small interest in these sordid romances had it not been that Madame Goldmarker had faithfully promised to look after Lisa and the twins, so that Mrs. Grubb might be free to hold classes in the adjoining towns. The little blind god had now overturned all these well-laid plans, and Mrs. Grubb was for the moment the victim of inexorable circumstances.

Dr. Boone fitted up princely apartments next his office, and Madame Goldmarker-Boone celebrated her nuptials and her desertion of Eden Place by making a formal début at a concert in Pocahontas Hall. The next morning, the neighborhood that knew them best, and many other neighborhoods that knew them not at all, received neat printed circulars thrust under the front door. Upon one side of the paper were printed the words and music of Home, Sweet Home "as sung by Madame Gold-marker-Boone at her late concert in Poca-hontas Hall." On the reverse side appeared a picture of the doctor, a neat cut of a human foot, a schedule of prices, and the alluring promise that the Madame's vocal pupils would receive treatment at half the regular rates.

Many small disputes and quarrels were consequent upon these business, emotional, and social convulsions, and each of the parties concerned, from Mrs. Grubb to the chiropodist, consulted Mistress Mary and solicited her advice and interference.

This seemed a little strange, but Mistress Mary's garden was the sort of place to act as a magnet to reformers, eccentrics, professional philanthropists, and cranks. She never quite understood the reason, and for that matter nobody else did, unless it were simply that the place was a trifle out of the common, and she herself a person full of ideas, and eminently sympathetic with those of other people. Anybody could "drop in," and as a consequence everybody did, — grandmothers, mothers with babes in arms, teachers, ministers, photographers, travelers, and journalists. A Russian gentleman who had escaped from Siberia was a frequent visitor. He wanted to marry Edith and open a boarding-house for Russian exiles, and was perfectly confident of making her happy, as he spoke seven languages and had been a good husband to two Russian ladies now deceased. An Alaskan missionary, home on a short leave, called periodically and attempted to persuade Mary to return with him to his heathen. These suitors were disposed of summarily when they made their desires known, but there were other visitors, part of the flotsam and jetsam of a great city, who appeared and disappeared mysteriously, — ships passing Mistress Mary in the night of sorrow, and, after some despairing, half-comprehended signal, vanishing into the shadows out of which they had come. Sometimes, indeed, inspired by the good cheer of the place, they departed looking a little less gloomy; sometimes, too, they grew into a kind of active if transitory relation with the busy little world, and became, for the time, a part of it.

Mistress Mary went down to the street corner with the children one noon to see them safely over the crossing. There was generally a genial policeman who made it a part of his duty to stand guard there, and guide the reckless and stupid and bewildered ones among the youngsters over the difficulties that lay in their path. Sometimes he would devote himself exclusively to Atlantic and Pacific Simonson, who really desired death, though they were not spiritually fitted for it, and bent all their energies toward getting under trucks rather than away from them. Marm Lisa never approached the spot without a nervous trembling and a look of terror in her eyes, and before the advent of the helpful officer had always taken a twin by each arm, and the three had gone over thus as a solid body, no matter how strong the resistance.

On this special morning there was no guardian of the peace in evidence, but standing on the crossing was a bearded man of perhaps forty years. Rather handsome he was, and well though carelessly dressed, but he stood irresolutely, with his hands in his pockets, as if quite undecided what to do next. Mary simply noted him as an altogether strange figure in the neighborhood, but the unexpected appearance of a large dog on the scene scattered the babies, and they fell on her in a weeping phalanx.

"Will you kindly help a little?" she asked after a moment's waiting, in which any chivalrous gentleman, she thought, should have flung himself into the breach.

"I?" he asked vaguely. "How do you mean? What shall I do?"

She longed to say, "Wake up, and perhaps an idea will come to you;" but she did say, with some spirit, "Almost anything, thank you. Drive the dog away, and help some of the smallest children across the street, please. You can have these two" (indicating the twins smilingly), "or the other ninety-eight, — whichever you like."

He obeyed orders, though not in a very alert fashion, but showed a sense of humor in choosing the ninety-eight rather than the two, and Mary left him on the corner with a pleasant word of thanks and a cheery remark.

The next morning he appeared at the garden gate, and asked if he might come in and sit awhile. He was made welcome; but it was a busy morning, and he was so silent a visitor that everybody forgot his existence.

He made a curious impression, which can hardly be described, save that any student of human nature would say at once, "He is out of relation with the world." He had something of the expression one sees in a recluse or a hermit. If you have ever wandered up a mountain side, you may have come suddenly upon a hut, a rude bed within it, and in the door a man reading, or smoking, or gazing into vacancy. You remember the look you met in that man's eyes. He has tasted life and found it bitter; has sounded the world and found it hollow; has known man or woman and found them false. Friendship to him is without savor, and love without hope.

After watching the children for an hour, the stranger slipped out quietly. Mistress Mary followed him to the door, abashed at her unintentional discourtesy in allowing him to go without a good-morning. She saw him stand at the foot of the steps, look first up, then down the street, then walk aimlessly to the corner. There, with hands in pockets, he paused again, glancing four ways; then, with a shrug and a gait that seemed to say, "It makes no difference," he slouched away.

"He is simply a stranger in a strange city, pining for his home," thought Mary, "or else he is a stranger in every city, and has nowhere a home."

He came again a few days later, and then again, apologizing for the frequency of his visits, but giving no special reason for them. The neophytes called him "the Solitary," but the children christened him after a fashion of their own, and began to ask small favors of him. "Thread my needle, please, Mr. Man!" "More beads," or "More paper, Mr. Man, please."

It is impossible to keep out of relation with little children. One of these mites of humanity would make a man out of your mountain hermit, resist as he might. They set up a claim on one whether it exists or not, and one has to allow it, and respond to it at least in some perfunctory fashion. More than once, as Mr. Man sat silently near the circle, the chubby Baker baby would fall over his feet, and he would involuntarily stoop to pick her up, straighten her dress, and soothe her woe. There was no hearty pleasure in his service even now. Nobody was certain that he felt any pleasure at all. His helpfulness was not spontaneous; it seemed a kind of reflex action, a survival of some former state of mind or heart; for he did his favors in a dream, nor heard any thanks, yet the elixir was working in his veins.

"He is dreadfully in the way," grumbled Edith; "he is more ever-present than my ardent Russian."

"So long as he insists on coming, let us make him supply the paternal element," suggested Rhoda. "It may be a degrading confession, but we could afford to part with several women here if we could only secure a really fatherly man. The Solitary cannot indulge in any day-dreams or trances, if we accept him as the patriarch of the institution."

Whereupon they boldly asked him, on his subsequent visits, to go upon errands, and open barrels of apples, and order intoxicated gentlemen off the steps, and mend locks and window-fastenings, and sharpen lead-pencils, and put on coal, and tell the lady in the rear that her parrot interfered with their morning prayers by shrieking the hymns in impossible keys. He accepted these tasks without protest, and performed them conscientiously, save in the parrot difficulty, in which case he gave one look at the lady, and fled without opening the subject.

It could not be said that he appeared more cheerful, the sole sign of any increased exhilaration of spirits being the occasional straightening of his cravat and the smoothing of his hair, — refinements of toilet that had heretofore been much neglected, though he always looked unmistakably the gentleman.

He seemed more attracted by Lisa than by any of the smaller children; but that may have been because Mary had told him her story, thinking that other people's stories were a useful sort of thing to tell people who had possible stories of their own.

Lisa was now developing a curious and unexpected facility and talent in the musical games. She played the tambourine, the triangle, the drum, as nobody else could, and in accompanying the marches she invented all sorts of unusual beats and accents. It grew to be the natural thing to give her difficult parts in the little dramas of child life: the cock that crowed in the morn to wake the sleeping birds and babies, the mother bird in the nest, the spreading willow-tree in the pond where the frogs congregated, — these rôles she delighted in and played with all her soul.

It would have been laughable, had it not been pathetic, to watch her drag Mr. Man into the games, and to see him succumb to her persuasions with his face hanging out flaming signals of embarrassment. In the "Carrier Doves" the little pigeons flew with an imaginary letter to him, and this meant that he was to stand and read it aloud, as Mary and Edith had done before him.

"It seems to be a letter from a child," he faltered, and then began stammeringly, "'My dear Mr. Man'"— There was a sudden stop. That there was a letter in his mind nobody could doubt, but he was too greatly moved to read it. Rhoda quickly reached out her hand for the paper, covering his discomfiture by exclaiming, "The pigeons have brought Mr. Man a letter from some children in his fatherland! Yes" (reading), "they hope that we will be good to him, because he is far away from home, and they send their love to all Mistress Mary's children. Wasn't it pretty of the doves to remember that Mr. Man is a stranger here?"

The Solitary appeared for the last time a week before Thanksgiving Day, and he opened the door on a scene of jollity that warmed him to the heart.

In the middle of the floor was a mimic boat, crowded from stem to stern with little Pilgrim fathers and mothers trying to land on Plymouth Rock, in a high state of excitement and an equally high sea. Pat Higgins was a chieftain commanding a large force of tolerably peaceful Indians on the shore, and Massasoit himself never exhibited more dignity; while Marm Lisa was the proud mother of the baby Oceanus born on the eventful voyage of the Mayflower.

Then Mistress Mary told the story of the festival very simply and sweetly, and all the tiny Pilgrims sang a hymn of thanksgiving. The Solitary listened, with his heart in his eyes and a sob in his throat; then, Heaven knows under the inspiration of what memory, he brushed Edith from the piano-stool, and seating himself in her place, played as if he were impelled by some irresistible force. The hand of a master had never swept those keys before, and he held his hearers spellbound.

There was a silence that could be felt.

The major part of the audience were not of an age to appreciate high art, but the youngsters were awed by the strange spectacle of Mr. Man at the piano, and with gaping mouth and strained ear listened to the divine harmonies he evoked. On and on he played, weaving the story of his past into the music, so it seemed to Mistress Mary. The theme came brokenly and uncertainly at first, as his thoughts strove for expression. Then out of the bitterness and gall, the suffering and the struggle, — and was it remorse? — was born a sweet, resolute, triumphant strain that carried the listeners from height to height of sympathy and emotion. It had not a hint of serenity; it was new-born courage, aspiration, and self-mastery, — the song of "him that overcometh."

When he paused, there was a deep-drawn breath, a sigh from hearts surcharged with feeling, and Lisa, who had drawn closer and closer to the piano, stood there now, one hand leaning on Mr. Man's shoulder and the tears chasing one another down her cheeks.

"It hurts me here," she sighed, pressing her hand to her heart.

He rose presently and left the room without a word, while the children prepared for home-going with a subdued air of having assisted at some solemn rite.

When Mistress Mary went out on the steps, a little later, he was still there.

"It is the last time! Auf wiedersehen!" he said.

"Auf wiedersehen," she answered gently, giving him her hand.

"Have you no Thanksgiving sermon for me?" he asked, holding her fingers lingeringly. "No child in all your flock needs it so much."

"Yes," said Mary, her eyes falling, for a moment, beneath his earnest gaze; but suddenly she lifted them again as she said bravely, "I have a sermon, but it is one with a trumpet-call, and little balm in it. 'Unto whomsoever anything is given, of him something shall be required.'"

When he reached the corner of the street he stopped, but instead of glancing four ways, as usual, he looked back at the porch where Mistress Mary stood. She carried Jenny Baker, a rosy sprig of babyhood, in the lovely curve of her arm, Bobby Baxter clasped her neck from behind in a strangling embrace, Johnny and Meg and Billy were tugging at her apron, and Marm Lisa was standing on tiptoe trying to put a rose in her hair. Then the Solitary passed into the crowd, and they saw him in the old places no more.

XIII.

LEAVES FROM MISTRESS MARY'S GARDEN.

"We have an unknown benefactor. A fortnight ago came three bushels of flowers: two hundred tiny nosegays marked 'For the children,' half a dozen knots of pink roses for the 'little mothers,' a dozen scarlet carnations for Lisa, while one great bunch of white lilies bore the inscription 'For the Mother Superior.' Last week a barrel of apples and another of oranges appeared mysteriously, and to-day comes a note, written in a hand we do not recognize, saying we are not to buy holly, mistletoe, evergreens, Christmas tree, or baubles of any kind, as they will be sent to us on December 22. We have inquired of our friends, but have no clew as yet, further than it must be somebody who knows our needs and desires very thoroughly. We have certainly entertained an angel unawares, but which among the crowd of visitors is it most likely to be? The Solitary, I wonder? I should

never have thought it, were it not for the
memory of that last day, the scene at the
piano, the 'song of him that overcometh,'
and the backward glance from the corner
as he sprang, absolutely sprang, on the car.
There was purpose in it, or I am greatly
mistaken. Mr. Man's eyes would be worth
looking into, if one could find purpose in
their brown depths! Moreover, though I
am too notorious a dreamer of dreams to be
trusted, I cannot help fancying he went *back*
to something; it was not a mere forward
move, not a sudden determination to find
some new duty to do that life might grow
nobler and sweeter, but a return to an old
duty grown hateful. That was what I saw
in his face as he stood on the crossing, with
the noon sunshine caught in his tawny hair
and beard. Rhoda, Edith, and I have each
made a story about him, and each of us
would vouch for the truth of her particular
version. I will not tell mine, but this is
Rhoda's; and while it differs from my own
in several important particulars, it yet bears
an astonishing resemblance to it. It is
rather romantic; but if one is to make any
sort of story out of the Solitary it must be
a romantic one, for he suggests no other.

"Rhoda began her tale with a thrilling introduction that set us all laughing (we smile here when still the tears are close at hand; indeed, we must smile, or we could not live): the prelude being something about a lonely castle in the heart of the Hartz Mountains, and a prattling golden-haired babe stretching its arms across a ruined moat in the direction of its absent father. This was in the nature of an absurd prologue, but when she finally came to the Solitary she grew serious; for she made him in the bygone days a sensitive child and a dreamy, impetuous youth, with a domineering, ill-tempered father who was utterly unable and unwilling to understand or to sympathize with him. His younger brother (for Rhoda insists on a younger brother) lived at home, while he, the elder, spent, or misspent, his youth and early manhood in a German university. As the years went on, the relations between himself and his father grew more and more strained. Do as the son might, he could never please, either in his line of thought and study or in his practical pursuits. The father hated his books, his music, his poetry, and his artist friends, while he on his part found nothing to stimulate or content him in his father's tasks and manner of life. His mother pined and died in the effort to keep peace between them, but the younger brother's schemes were quite in an opposite direction. At this time Mr. Man flung himself into a foolish marriage, one that promised little in the shape of the happiness he craved so eagerly. (Rhoda insists on this unhappy marriage; I am in doubt about it.) Finally his father died, and on being summoned home, as he supposed, to take his rightful place and assume the management of the estate, he found himself disinherited. He could have borne the loss of fortune and broad acres better than this convincing proof of his father's dislike and distrust, and he could have endured even that, had it not befallen him through the perfidy of his brother. When, therefore, he was met by his wife's bitter reproaches and persistent coldness, he closed his heart against all the world, shook the dust of home from off his feet, left his own small fortune behind him, kissed his little son, and became a wanderer on the face of the earth.

"This is substantially Rhoda's story, but

it does not satisfy her completely. She says, in her whimsical way, that it needs another villain to account properly for Mr. Man's expression.

"Would it not be strange if by any chance we have brought him to a happier frame of mind? Would it not be a lovely tribute to the secret power of this place, to the healing atmosphere of love that we try to create, — that atmosphere in which we bathe our own tired spirits day by day, re-creating ourselves with every new dawn? But whether our benefactor be the Solitary or not, some heart has been brought into new relation with us and with the world. It only confirms my opinion that everybody is at his or her best in the presence of children. In what does the magic of their influence consist? This morning I was riding down in the horse-cars, and a poor ragged Italian woman entered, a baby in her arms, and two other children following close behind. The girl was a mite of a thing, prematurely grave, serious, pretty, and she led a boy just old enough to toddle. She lifted him carefully up to the seat (she who should have been lifted herself!), took his hat, smoothed his damp curly hair, and tucked his head down on her shoulder, a shoulder that had begun its life-work full early, poor tot! The boy was a feeble, frail, ill-nourished, dirty young urchin, who fell asleep as soon as his head touched her arm. His child nurse, having made him comfortable, gave a sigh of relief, and looked up and down the car with a radiant smile of content. Presto, change! All the railroad magnates and clerks had been watching her over their newspapers, and in one instant she had captured the car. I saw tears in many eyes, and might have seen more had not my own been full. There was apparently no reason for the gay, winsome, enchanting smile that curved the red mouth, brought two dimples into the brown cheeks, and sunny gleams into two dark eyes. True, she was riding instead of walking, and her charge was sleeping instead of waking and wailing; but these surely were trifling matters on which to base such rare content. Yet there it was shining in her face as she met a dozen pairs of eyes, and saw in each of them love for her sweet motherly little self, and love for the 'eternal womanly' of which she was the visible expression. There was a general exodus at Brett Street, and every man furtively slipped a piece of silver into the child's lap as he left the car; each, I think, trying to hide his action from the others.

"It is of threads such as these that I weave the fabric of my daily happiness, — a happiness that my friends never seem able to comprehend; the blindest of them pity me, indeed, but I consider myself, like Mary of old, ' blessed among women.' "

.   .   .   .

Another day. — "God means all sorts of things when he sends men and women into the world. That he means marriage, and that it is the chiefest good, I have no doubt, but it is the love forces in it that make it so. I may, perhaps, reach my highest point of development without marriage, but I can never do it unless I truly and deeply love somebody or something. I am not sure, but it seems to me God intends me for other people's children, not for my own. My heart is so entirely in my work that I fancy I have none left for a possible hus-band. If ever a man comes who is strong enough and determined enough to sweep things aside and make a place for himself, willy-nilly, I shall ask him to come in and rest; but that seems very unlikely. What man have I ever seen who would help me to be the woman my work helps me to be? Of course there are such, but the Lord keeps them safely away from my humble notice, lest I should die of love or be guilty of hero-worship.

"Men are so dull, for the most part! They are often tender and often loyal, but they seldom put any spiritual leaven into their tenderness, and their loyalty is apt to be rather unimaginative. Heigho! I wish we could make lovers as the book-writers do, by rolling the virtues and graces of two or three men into one! I'd almost like to be a man in this decade, a young, strong man, for there are such splendid giants to slay! To be sure, a woman can always buckle on the sword, and that is rather a delightful avocation, after all; but somehow there are comparatively few men nowadays who care greatly to wear swords or have them buckled on. There is no inspiration in trying to buckle on the sword of a man who never saw one, and who uses it wrong end foremost, and falls down on it, and entangles his legs in it, and scratches his lady's hand with it whenever he kisses her!

And therefore, these things, for aught I see, being unalterably so, I will take children's love, woman's love, and man's friendship; man's friendship, which, if it is not life's poetry, is credible prose, says George Meredith, — 'a land of low undulations, instead of Alps, beyond the terrors and deceptions.' That will fill to overflowing my life, already so full, and in time I shall grow from everybody's Mistress Mary into everybody's Mother Mary, and that will be the end of me in my present state of being. I am happy, yes, I am blessedly happy in this prospect, and yet" —

．　　．　　．　　．　　．　　．　　．

Another day. — "My beloved work! How beautiful it is! Toniella has not brought little Nino this week. She says he is ill, but that he sits every day in the orchard, singing our songs and modeling birds from the lump of clay we sent him. When I heard that phrase ' in the orchard,' I felt a curious sensation, for I know they live in a tenement house; but I said nothing, and went to visit them.

"The orchard is a few plants in pots and pans on a projecting window-sill!

"My heart went down on its knees when

I saw it. The divine spark is in those children; it will be a moving power, helping them to struggle out of their present environment into a wider, sunnier one, — the one of the real orchards. How fresh, how full of possibilities, is the world to the people who can keep the child heart, and above all to the people who are able to see orchards in window-boxes!"

.   .   .   .

Another day. — "Lisa's daily lesson is just finished. It was in arithmetic, and I should have lost patience had it not been for her musical achievements this morning. Edith played the airs of twenty or thirty games, and without a word of help from us she associated the right memory with each, and illustrated it with pantomime. In some cases, she invented gestures of her own that showed deeper intuition than ours; and when, last of all, the air of the Carrier Doves was played, a vision of our Solitary must have come before her mind. Her lip trembling, she held an imaginary letter in her fingers, and, brushing back the hair from her forehead (his very gesture!), she passed her hand across her eyes, laid the make-believe note in Rhoda's apron, and slipped out of the door without a word.

"'Mr. Man! Mr. Man! It is Mr. Man when he could n't read his letter!' cried the children. 'Why does n't he come to see us any more, Miss Rhoda?'

"'He is doing some work for Miss Mary, I think,' answered Rhoda, with a teasing look at me.

"Lisa came back just then, and rubbed her cheek against my arm. 'I went to the corner,' she whispered, 'but he was n't there; he is never there now!'

"It was the remembrance of this astonishing morning that gave me courage in the later lesson. She seems to have no idea of numbers, — there will be great difficulty there, — but she begins to read well, and the marvel of it is that she has various talents! She is weak, uneducated; many things are either latent or altogether missing in her as yet, and I do not know how many of them will appear, nor how long a process it will be; but her mind is full of compensations, and that is the last thing I expected. It is only with infinite struggle that she *learns* anything, though she is capable of struggle, and that is a good deal to say; but she has besides a precious heritage of instincts and insights, hitherto unsus-

pected and never drawn upon. It is precisely as if there had been a bundle of possibilities folded away somewhere in her
brain, but hidden by an intervening veil, or
crushed by some alien weight. We seem
to have drawn away that curtain or lifted
that weight, and the faculties so long ob-
scured are stretching themselves and growing with their new freedom. · It reminds
me of the weak, stunted grass blades under
a stone. I am always lifting it and rolling
it away, sentimentally trying to give the
struggling shoots a chance. One can see
for many a long day where the stone has
been, but the grass forgets it after a while,
when it breathes the air and sunshine, tastes
the dew and rain, and feels the miracle of
growth within its veins."

.   .   .   .   .   .

Another day. — "The twins are certainly
improving a trifle. They are by no means
angelic, but they are at least growing human; and if ever their tremendous energy
— a very whirlwind — is once turned in the
right direction, we shall see things move, I
warrant you! Rhoda says truly that the
improvement cannot be seen with the naked
eye; but the naked eye is never in use with

us, in our work, nor indeed with the Father of Lights, who teaches us all to see truly if we will.

"The young minister has spent a morning with us. He came to make my acquaintance, shook me warmly by the hand, and — that was the last I saw of him, for he kept as close to Rhoda's side as circumstances would permit! The naked eye is all one needs to discern his motives! Psychological observations, indeed! Child study, forsooth! It was lovely to see Rhoda's freshness, spontaneity, and unconsciousness, as she flitted about like a pretty cardinal-bird. Poor young minister, whose heart is dangling at the strings of her scarlet apron! Lucky young minister, if his arm ever goes about that slender red-ribboned waist, and his lips ever touch that glowing cheek! But poor me! what will the garden be without our crimson rose?"

XIV.

MORE LEAVES.

"It has been one of the discouraging days. Lisa was willful; the twins had a moral relapse; the young minister came again, and, oh, the interminable length of time he held Rhoda's hand at parting! Is it not strange that, with the whole universe to choose from, his predatory eye must fall upon my blooming Rhoda? I wonder whether the fragrance she will shed upon that one small parsonage will be as widely disseminated as the sweetness she exhales here, day by day, among our 'little people all in a row?' I am not sure; I hope so; at any rate, selfishness must not be suffered to eclipse my common sense, and the young minister seems a promising, manly fellow.

"When we have had a difficult day, I go home and sit down in my cosy corner in the twilight, the time and place where I always repeat my *credo*, which is this: —

"It is the children of this year, of every

new year, who are to bring the full dawn, that dawn that has been growing since first the world began. It is not only that children re-create the world year by year, decade by decade, by making over human nature; by transforming trivial, thoughtless men and women into serious, earnest ones; by waking in arid natures slumbering seeds of generosity, self-sacrifice, and helpfulness. It is not alone in this way that children are bringing the dawn of the perfect day. It is the children (bless them! how naughty they were to-day!) who are going to do all we have left undone, all we have failed to do, all we might have done had we been wise enough, all we have been too weak and stupid to do.

"Among the thousands of tiny things growing up all over the land, some of them under my very wing, — watched and tended, unwatched and untended, loved, unloved, protected from danger, thrust into temptation, — among them somewhere is the child who will write a great poem that will live forever and ever, kindling every generation to a loftier ideal. There is the child who will write the novel that is to stir men's hearts to nobler issues and incite them to

better deeds. There is the child (perhaps
it is Nino) who will paint the greatest picture or carve the greatest statue of the age;
another who will deliver his country in an
hour of peril; another who will give his life
for a great principle; and another, born
more of the spirit than the flesh, who will
live continually on the heights of moral
being, and dying, draw men after him. It
may be I shall preserve one of these children to the race, — who knows? It is a
peg big enough on which to hang a hope,
for every child born into the world is a new
incarnate thought of God, an ever fresh and
radiant possibility."

· · · · · · ·

Another day. — "Would I had the gift
to capture Mrs. Grubb and put her between
the covers of a book!

"It tickles Rhoda's fancy mightily that
the Vague Lady (as we call her) should take
Lisa before the Commissioners of Lunacy!
Rhoda says that if she has an opportunity
to talk freely with them, they will inevitably jump at the conclusion that Lisa has
brought *her* for examination, as she is so
much the more irrational of the two! Rhoda
facetiously imagines a scene in which a rev-

erend member of the body takes Lisa aside and says solemnly, 'My dear child, you have been wise beyond your years in bringing us your guardian, and we cannot allow her to be at large another day, lest she become suddenly violent.'

"Of late I have noticed that she has gradually dropped one club and society after another, concentrating her attention more and more upon Theosophy. Every strange weed and sucker that can grow anywhere flourishes in the soil of her mind, and if a germ of truth or common sense does chance to exist in any absurd theory, it is choked by the time it has lain there among the underbrush for a little space; so that when she begins her harvesting (which is always a long while before anything is ripe), one can never tell precisely what sort of crop was planted.

"It seems that the Theosophists are considering the establishment of a colony of Mahatmas at Mojave, on the summit of the Tehachapi Mountains. Their present habitat is the Himalayas, but there is no reason why we should not encourage them to settle in this country. The Tehachapis would give as complete retirement as the Hima-

layas, while the spiritual advantages to be
derived from an infusion of Mahatmas into
our population is self-evident. 'Think, my
sisters,' Mrs. Grubb would say, 'think,
that our mountain ranges may some time
be peopled by omniscient beings thousands
of years old and still growing!' Up to this
last aberration I have had some hope of
Grubb o' Dreams. I thought it a good
sign, her giving up so many societies and
meetings. The house is not any tidier, but
at least she stays in it occasionally. In the
privacy of my own mind I have been ascrib-
ing this slight reformation to the most ordinary cause, — namely, a Particular Man.
It would never have occurred to me in her
case had not Edith received confidential
advices from Mrs. Sylvester.

"'We're going to lose her, I feel it!'
said Mrs. Sylvester. 'I feel it, and she
alludes to it herself. There ain't but two
ways of her classes losing her, death and
marriage; and as she looks too healthy to
die, it must be the other one. She's never
accepted any special attentions till about a
month ago, when the Improved Order of
Red Men held their Great Council here.
You see she used to be Worthy Wenonah

of Pocahontas Lodge years ago, when my husband was Great Keeper of the Wampum, but she has n't attended regularly; a woman is so handicapped, when it comes to any kind of public work, by her home and her children. — I do hope I shall live long enough to see all those kind of harassing duties performed in public, coöperative institutions. — She went to the Council to keep me company, mostly, but the very first evening I could see that William Burkhardt, of Bald Eagle No. 62, was struck with her; she lights up splendidly, Mrs. Grubb does. He stayed with her every chance he got during the week: but I did n't see her give him any encouragement, and I should never have thought of it again if she had n't come home late from one of the Council Fires at the Wigwam. I was just shutting my bedroom blinds. I tried not to listen, for I despise eavesdropping, of all things, but I could n't help hearing her say, "No, Mr. Burkhardt, you are only a Junior Sagamore, and I am ambitious. When you are a Great Sachem, it will be time enough to consider the matter.'"

"Mrs. Sylvester, Edith, and I agreed that this was most significant, but we may

have been mistaken, according to her latest
development. The 'passing away' so feel-
ingly alluded to by Mrs. Sylvester is to be
of a different sort. She has spoken mysteriously to me before of her reasons for denying herself luxuries; of the goal she expected to reach through rigid denial of the
body and training of the spirit; of her longing to come less in contact with the foul
magnetism of the common herd, so detri-
mental to her growth; but she formally announced to me in strict confidence to-day
her ambition to be a Mahatma. Of course
she has been so many things that there are
comparatively few left; still, say whatever
we like, she has the spirit of all the Argo-
nauts, that woman! She has been an Ini-
tiate for some time, and considers herself
quite ready for the next step, which is to be
a Chela. It is unnecessary to state that
she climbs the ladder of evolution much
faster than the ordinary Theosophist, who is
somewhat slow in his movements, and often
deals in centuries, or even æons.

"I did not know that there were female
Mahatmas, reasoning unconsciously from
the fact that an Adept is supposed to hold
his peace for many years before he can even

contemplate the possibility of being a Mahatma. (The idea of Grubb o' Dreams holding her peace is too absurd for argument.) There are many grades of Adepts, it seems, ranging from the 'topmost' Mahatmas down. The highest of all, the Nirmanakayas, are self-conscious without the body, traveling hither and thither with but one object, that of helping humanity. As we descend the scale, we find Adepts (and a few second-class Mahatmas) living in the body, for the wheel of Karma has not entirely revolved for them; but they have a key to their 'prison' (that is what Mrs. Grubb calls her nice, pretty body!), and can emerge from it at pleasure. That is, any really capable and energetic Adept can project his soul from its prison to any place that he pleases, with the rapidity of thought. I may have my personal doubts as to the possibilities of this gymnastic feat, but Mrs. Grubb's intellectual somersaults have been of such thoroughness and frequency that I am sure, if anybody can perform the gyration, she can! Meantime, there are decades of retirement, meditation, and preparation necessary, and she can endure nothing of that sort in this present incarnation, so the parting does not seem imminent!

"She came to consult me about Soul Haven for the twins. I don't think it a wholly bad plan. The country is better for them than the city; we can manage to get occasional news of their welfare; it will tide over the brief interval of time needed by Mrs. Grubb for growing into a Chela; and in any event, they are sure to run away from the Haven as soon as they become at all conscious of their souls, a moment which I think will be considerably delayed.

"Mrs. Grubb will not yield Lisa until she is certain that the Soul Haven colonists will accept the twins without a caretaker, but unless the matter is quietly settled by the new year I shall find some heroic means of changing her mind. I have considered the matter earnestly for many months without knowing precisely how to find sufficient money for the undertaking. My own income can be stretched to cover her maintenance, but it is not sufficient to give her the proper sort of education. She is beyond my powers now, and perhaps — nay, of a certainty, if her health continues to improve — five years of skillful teaching will make her — what it will make her no one can prophesy, but it is sure to be something worth working for. No doubt I can get the money by a public appeal, and if it were for a dozen children instead of one, I would willingly do it, as indeed I have done it many times in the past.

"That was a beautiful thought of Pastor Von Bodelschwingh, of the Colony of Mercy in Germany. 'Mr. Man' told me about him in one of the very few long talks we had together. He had a home for adults and children of ailing mind and body, and when he wanted a new house for the little ones, and there was no money to build or equip it, he asked every parent in Germany for a thank-offering to the Lord of one penny for each well child. Within a short fortnight four hundred thousand pennies flowed in, — four hundred thousand thank-offerings for children strong and well. The good pastor's wish was realized, and his Baby Castle an accomplished fact. Not only did the four hundred thousand pennies come, but the appeal for them stimulated a new sense of gratitude among all the parents who responded, so that there came pretty, touching messages from all sides, such as: 'Four pennies for four living children; for a child in heaven, two.' 'Six pennies for a happy home.' 'One penny for the child we never had.' 'Five pennies for a good wife.'

"Ah! never, surely, was a Baby Castle framed of such lovely timber as this! It seems as if heaven's sweet air must play about the towers, and heaven's sunshine stream in at every window, of a house built from turret to foundation-stone of such royal material. The Castle might look like other castles, but every enchanted brick and stone and block of wood, every grain of mortar, every bit of glass and marble, un-like all others of its kind, would be trans-formed by the thought it represented and thrilled with the message it bore.

"Such an appeal I could make for my whole great family, but somehow this seems almost a private matter, and I am sensitive about giving it publicity. My love and hope for Lisa are so great I cannot bear to describe her 'case,' nor paint her unhappy childhood in the hues it deserves, for the sake of gaining sympathy and aid. I may have to do it, but would I were the little Crœsus of a day! Still, Christmas is com-ing, and who knows?

'Everywhere the Feast o' the Babe,
Joy upon earth, peace and good-will to men!
We are baptized.'

Merry Christmas is coming. Everybody's hand-grasp is warmer because of it, though of course it is the children whose merriment rings truest.

"There are just one or two things, grown up as I am, that I should like to find in the toe of my stocking on Christmas morning; only they are impalpable things that could neither be put in nor taken out of real stockings.

"Old as we are, we are most of us mere children in this, that we go on hoping that next Christmas all the delicious happenings we have missed in other Christmases may descend upon us by the old and reliable chimney route! A Santa Claus that had any bowels of compassion would rush down the narrowest and sootiest chimney in the world to give me my simple wishes. It is n't as if I were petitioning nightly for a grand house, a yacht, a four-in-hand, a diamond necklace, and a particular man for a husband; but I don't see that modesty finds any special favor with St. Nick. Now and then I harbor a rascally suspicion that he is an indolent, time-serving person, who slips down the widest, cleanest chimneys to the people who clamor the loudest; but this abominable cynicism melts into thin air the moment that I look at his jolly visage on the cover of a picture-book. Dear, fat, rosy, radiant Being! Surely he is incapable of any but the highest motives! I am twenty-eight years old, but age shall never make any difference in the number or extent of my absurdities. I am going to write a letter and send it up the chimney! It never used to fail in the long-ago; but ah! then there were two dear, faithful go-betweens to interpret my childish messages of longing to Santa Claus, and jog his memory at the critical time!"

XV.

"THE FEAST O' THE BABE."

IT was sure to be a green Christmas in that sunny land, but not the sort of "green Yule" that makes the "fat kirkyard." If the New Englanders who had been transplanted to that shore of the Pacific ever longed for a bracing snowstorm, for frost pictures on the window-panes, for the breath of a crystal air blown over ice-fields, — an air that nipped the ears, but sent the blood coursing through the veins, and made the turkey and cranberry sauce worth eating, — the happy children felt no lack, and basked contentedly in the soft December sunshine. Still farther south there were mothers who sighed even more for the sound of merry sleigh-bells, the snapping of logs on the hearth, the cosy snugness of a firelit room made all the snugger by the fierce wind without; that, if you like, was a place to hang a row of little red and brown woolen stockings! And when the fortunate chil-

dren on the eastern side of the Rockies,
tired with resisting the Sand Man, had
snuggled under the great down comforters
and dropped off to sleep, they dreamed, of
course, of the proper Christmas things, —
of the tiny feet of reindeer pattering over
the frozen crust, the tinkle of silver bells
on their collars, the real Santa Claus with
icicles in his beard, with red cheeks, and a
cold nose, and a powder of snow on his
bearskin coat, and with big fur mittens
never too clumsy to take the toys from his
pack.

Here the air blew across orange groves
and came laden with the sweetness of opening buds; here, if it were a sunny Christmas Day, as well it might be, the children
came in to dinner tired with playing in the
garden: but the same sort of joyous cries
that rent the air three thousand miles away
at sight of hot plum pudding woke the
echoes here because of fresh strawberries
and loquats; and although, in the minds of
the elders, who had been born in snowdrifts
and bred upon icicles, this union of balmy
air, singing birds, and fragrant bloom might
strike a false note at Christmastide, it
brought nothing but joy to the children.

After all, if it were not for old association's sake, it would seem that one might fitly celebrate the birthday of the Christ-child under sunshine as warm and skies of the same blue as those that sheltered the heavenly Babe in old Judea.

During the late days of October and the early days of November the long drought of summer had been broken, and it had rained steadily, copiously, refreshingly. Since then there had been day after day of brilliant, cloudless sunshine, and the moist earth, warmed gratefully through to the marrow, stirred and trembled and pushed forth myriads of tender shoots from the seeds that were hidden in its bosom; and the tender shoots themselves looked up to the sun, and, with their roots nestled in sweet, fragrant beds of richness, thought only of growing tall and green, dreamed only of the time when pink pimpernels would bloom between their waving blades, and when tribes of laughing children would come to ramble over the hillsides. The streets of the city were full of the fragrance of violets, for the flower-venders had great baskets of them over their arms, and on every corner tempted the passers-by with

the big odorous purple bunches that offered
a royal gift of sweetness for every penny
invested.

Atlantic and Pacific Simonson had previously known little, and Marm Lisa less,
of Christmas time, but the whole month of
December in Mistress Mary's garden was
a continual feast of the new-born Babe.
There was an almost oppressive atmosphere
of secrecy abroad. Each family of children, working in the retirement of its particular corner, would shriek, "Oh, don't
come!" and hide small objects under pina-
fores and tables when Mary, Rhoda, Edith,
or Helen appeared. The neophyte in charge
was always in the attitude of a surprised
hen, extending her great apron to its utmost
area as a screen to hide these wonderful
preparations. Edith's group was slaving
over Helen's gift, Rhoda's over Edith's,
and so on, while all the groups had some
marvelous bit of coöperative work in hand
for Mistress Mary. At the afternoon council, the neophytes were obliged to labor conscientiously on presents destined for themselves, rubbing off stains, disentangling
knots, joining threads, filling up wrong
holes and punching right ones, surrepti-

tiously getting the offerings of love into a condition where the energetic infants could work on them again. It was somewhat difficult to glow and pale with surprise when they received these well-known and well-worn trophies of skill from the tree at the proper time, but they managed to achieve it.

Never at any other season was there such scrubbing of paws, and in spite of the most devoted sacrifices to the Moloch of cleanliness the excited little hands grew first moist, and then grimy, nobody knew how. "It must leak out of the inside of me," wailed Bobby Baxter when sent to the pump for the third time one morning; but he went more or less cheerfully, for his was the splendid honor of weaving a frame for Lisa's picture, and he was not the man to grudge an inch or two of skin if thereby he might gain a glorious immortality.

The principal conversation during this festival time consisted of phrases like: "I know what you 're goin' to have, Miss Edith, but I won't tell!" "Miss Mary, Sally 'most told Miss Rhoda what she was makin' for her." "Miss Helen, Pat Higgins went right up to Miss Edith and asked her to help him mend the leg of his clay frog, and it's his own Christmas present for her!"

The children could not for the life of them play birds, or butterflies, or carpenter, or scissors-grinder, for they wanted to shout the livelong day, —

> " Christmas bells are ringing sweet,
>   We too the happy day must greet ; "

or, —

> " Under the holly, now,
>   Sing and be jolly, now,
> Christmas has come and the children are glad ; "

or, —

> " Hurrah for Santa Claus !
> Long may he live at his castle in Somewhere-land !

There was much whispering and discussion about evergreens and garlands and wreaths that were soon to come, and much serious planning with regard to something to be made for mother, father, sister, brother, and the baby; something, too, now and then, for a grandpapa in Sweden, a grandmamma in Scotland, a Norwegian uncle, an Irish aunt, and an Italian cousin; but there was never by chance any cogitation as to what the little workers themselves might get. In the happier homes among them, there was doubtless the usual legitimate speculation as to doll or drum, but here in this enchanted spot, this materialized Altruria, the talk was all of giving, when the Wonderful Tree bloomed in their midst, — the Wonderful Tree they sang about every morning, with the sweet voice

> "telling its branches among
> Of shepherd's watch and of angel's song,
> Of lovely Babe in manger low, —
> The beautiful story of long ago,
> When a radiant star threw its beams so wide
> To herald the earliest Christmastide."

The Tree was coming, — Mistress Mary said so; and bless my heart, you might possibly meddle with the revolution of the earth around the sun, or induce some weak-minded planet to go the wrong way, but you would be helpless to reverse one of Mistress Mary's promises! They were as fixed and as unchangeable as the laws of the Medes and Persians, and there was a record of their fulfillment indelibly written in the memories of two hundred small personages, — personages in whom adult caprice and flexibility of conduct had bred a tendency to suspicion.

The Tree, therefore, had been coming for a fortnight, and on the 22d it came! Neither did it come alone, for it was accompanied by a forest of holly and mistletoe, and ropes of evergreen, and wreaths and garlands of laurel, and green stars by the dozen. And in a great box, at present hidden from the children, were heaps of candles, silver and crystal baubles, powdered snowflakes, glass icicles, gilded nuts, party-colored spheres, cornucopias full of goodies, and, above all, two wonderful Christmas angels and a snow-white dove!

Neither tree, nor garlands, nor box contained any hint of the donor, to the great disappointment of the neophytes. Rhoda had an idea, for Cupid had "clapped her i' the shoulder," and her intuitions were preternaturally keen just now. Mary almost knew, though she had never been in love in her life, and her faculties were working only in their every-day fashion; but she was not in the least surprised when she drew a letter from under the white dove's wing. Seeing that it was addressed to her, she waited until everybody had gone, and sat under the pepper-tree in the deserted playground where she might read it in solitude.

"Dear Mistress Mary," it said, "do you care to hear of my life?

'Das Ewig-Weibliche
Zieht uns hinan,'

and I am growing olives. Do you remember what the Spanish monk said to the tree that he pruned, and that cried out under his hook? 'It is not beauty that is wanted of you, nor shade, but olives.' The sun is hot, and it has not rained for many a long week, it seems to me, but the dew of your influence falls ever sweet and fresh on the dust of my daily task.

"Inclosed please find the wherewithal for Lisa's next step higher. As she needs more it will come. I give it for sheer gratitude, as the good folk gave their pennies to Pastor Von Bodelschwingh. Why am I grateful? For your existence, to be sure! I had lived my life haunted by the feeling that there was such a woman, and finally the mysterious wind of destiny blew me to her, ' as the tempest brings the rose-tree to the pollard willow.'

"Do not be troubled about me, little mother-of-many! There was once upon a time a common mallow by the roadside, and being touched by Mohammed's garment as he passed it was changed at once into a geranium; and best of all, it remained a geranium forever after.

"Your Solitary."

XVI.

CLEANSING FIRES.

It was the afternoon of the day before Christmas, and all the little people had gone home, leaving the room vacant for the decking of the Wonderful Tree. Edith, Helen, and others were perched on step-ladders, festooning garlands and wreaths from window to window, and post to post. Mary and Rhoda were hanging burdens of joy among the green branches of the tree.

The room began to look more and more lovely as the evergreen stars were hung by scarlet ribbons in each of the twelve windows, and the picture-frames were crowned with holly branches. Then Mistress Mary was elevated to a great height on a pyramid of tables and chairs, and suspended the two Christmas angels by invisible wires from the ceiling. When the chorus of admiration had subsided, she took the white dove tenderly from Rhoda's upstretched hands (and what a charming Christmas picture they made, — the eager upturned rosy face of the one, the gracious fairness of the other!) and laying its soft breast against her cheek for a moment, perched it on the topmost branch of waving green with a thought of "Mr. Man," and a hope that the blessed day might bring him a tithe of the cheer he had given them. The effect of the dove and the angels was so electrical that all the fresh young voices burst into the chorus of the children's hymn: —

> He was born upon this day
> In David's town so far away,
> He the good and loving One,
> Mary's ever-blessèd Son.
> Let us all our voices lend,
> For He was the children's Friend,
> He so lovely, He so mild,
> Jesus, blessed Christmas Child!

As the last line of the chorus floated through the open windows, an alarm of fire sounded, followed by a jangle of bells and a rumble of patrol wagons. On going to the west window, Edith saw a blaze of red light against the sky, far in the distance, in the direction of Lone Mountain. Soon after, almost on the heels of the first, came another alarm, with its attendant clangings, its cries of "Fire!" its chatterings and conjectures, its rushing of small boys in all directions, its tread of hurrying policemen, its hasty flinging up of windows and grouping of heads therein.

The girls were too busy labeling the children's gifts to listen attentively to the confused clamor in the streets, — fires were common enough in a city built of wood; but when, half an hour after the first and second alarms, a third sounded, they concluded it must be a conflagration, and Rhoda, dropping her nuts and cornucopias, ran to the corner for news. She was back again almost immediately, excited and breathless.

"Oh, Mary!" she exclaimed, her hand on her panting side, "unless they are mistaken, it is three separate fires: one, a livery-stable and carriage-house out towards Lone Mountain; another fearful one on Telegraph Hill, — a whole block of houses, and they have n't had enough help there because of the Lone Mountain fire; now there 's a third alarm, and they say it 's at the corner of Sixth and Dutch streets. If it is, we have a tenement house next door; is n't that clothing-place on the corner? Yes, I know it is; make haste! Edith and Helen will watch the Christmas things."

Mary did not need to be told to hasten. She had her hat in her hand and was on the sidewalk before Rhoda had fairly finished her sentence.

They hurried through the streets, guided by the cloud of smoke that gushed from the top of a building in the near distance. Almost everybody was running in the opposite direction, attracted by the Telegraph Hill fire that flamed vermilion and gold against the gray sky, looking from its elevation like a mammoth bonfire, or like a hundred sunsets massed in one lurid pile of color.

"Is it the Golden Gate tenement house?" they asked of the neighborhood locksmith, who was walking rapidly towards them.

"No, it's the coat factory next door," he answered, hurriedly. "'T would n't be so much of a blaze if they could get the fire company here to put it out before it gets headway; but it's one o' those blind fires that's been sizzling away inside the walls for an hour. The folks did n't know they was afire till a girl ran in and told 'em, — your Lisa it was, — and they did n't believe her at first; but it war n't a minute before the flames burst right through the plastering in half a dozen places to once. I tell you they just dropped everything where it was and run for their lives. There war n't but one man on the premises, and he was such a blamed fool he wasted five minutes trying to turn the alarm into the letter-box on the lamp-post, 'stead of the right one alongside. I 'm going home for some tools — Hullo! there 's the flames coming through one corner o' the roof; that 's the last o' the factory, I guess; but it ain't much loss, anyway; it 's a reg'lar sweatin'-shop. They 'll let it go now, and try to save the buildings each side of it, — that 's what they 'll do."

That is what they were doing when Mary and Rhoda broke away from the voluble locksmith in the middle of his discourse and neared the scene of excitement. The firemen had not yet come, though it was rumored that a detachment was on the way. All the occupants of the tenement house were taking their goods and chattels out, — running down the narrow stairways with feather-beds, dropping clocks and china ornaments from the windows, and endangering their lives by crawling down the fire-escapes with small articles of no value. Men were scarce at that hour in that locality, but there was a good contingent of small shopkeepers and gentlemen-of-steady-leisure, who were on the roof pouring water over wet blankets and comforters and carpets. A crazy-looking woman in the fourth story kept dipping a child's handkerchief in and out of a bowl of water and wrapping it about a tomato-can with a rosebush planted in it. Another, very much intoxicated, leaned from her window, and, regarding the whole matter as an agreeable entertainment, called down humorous remarks and ribald jokes to the oblivious audience. There was an improvised hook-and-ladder company pouring water where it was least needed, and a zealous self-appointed commanding officer who did nothing but shout contradictory orders; but as nobody obeyed them, and every man did just as he was inclined, it did not make any substantial difference in the result.

Mary and Rhoda made their way through the mass of interested spectators, not so many here as on the cooler side of the street. Where was Lisa? That was the first, indeed the only question. How had she come there? Where had she gone? There was a Babel of confusion, but nothing like the uproar that would have been heard

had not part of the district's population fled
to the more interesting fire, and had not the
whole thing been so quiet and so lightning-
quick in its progress. The whole scene now
burst upon their view. A few harassed
policemen had stretched ropes across the
street, and were trying to keep back the
rebellious ones in the crowd who ever and
anon would struggle under the line and have
to be beaten back by force.

As Mary and Rhoda approached, a group
on the outskirts cried out, "Here she is!
'T ain't more 'n a minute sence they went to
tell her! Here she is now!"

The expected fire brigade could hardly
be called "she," Mary thought, as she
glanced over her shoulder. She could see
no special reason for any interest in her own
movements. She took advantage of the
parting of the crowd, however, and as she
made her way she heard, as in a waking
dream, disjointed sentences that had no
meaning at first, but being pieced together
grew finally into an awful whole.

"Why did n't the factory girls bring 'em
out? Did n't know they was there?"

"Say, one of 'em was saved, war n't it?"

"Which one of 'em did she get down
before the roof caught?"

"No, 't ain't no such thing; the manager's across the bay; she gave the alarm herself."

"She did n't know they was in there; I bet yer they 'd run and hid, and she was hunting 'em when she seen the smoke."

"Yes, she did; she dropped the girl twin out the second-story window into Abe Isaac's arms, but she did n't know the boy was in the building till just now, and they can't hardly hold her."

"She 's foolish, anyhow, ain't she?"

Mary staggered beyond Rhoda to the front of the crowd.

"Let me under the rope!" she cried, with a mother's very wail in her tone, — "let me under the rope, for God's sake! They 're my children!"

At this moment she heard a stentorian voice call to some one, "Wait a minute till the firemen get here, and they 'll go for him! Come back, girl, d—n you! you shan't go!"

"Wait? No! *Not* wait!" cried Lisa, tearing herself dexterously from the policeman's clutches, and dashing like a whirlwind up the tottering stairway before any one else could gather presence of mind to seize and detain her.

Pacific was safe on the pavement, but she had only a moment before been flung from those flaming windows, and her terrified shrieks rent the air. The crowd gave a long-drawn groan, and mothers turned their eyes away and shivered. Nobody followed Marm Lisa up that flaming path of death and duty: it was no use flinging a good life after a worthless one.

"Fool! crazy fool!" people ejaculated, with tears of reverence in their eyes.

"Darling, splendid fool!" cried Mary. "Fool worth all the wise ones among us!"

"He that loseth his life for my sake shall find it!" said a pious Methodist cobbler with a patched boot under his arm.

In the eternity of waiting that was numbered really but in seconds, a burly policeman beckoned four men and gave them a big old-fashioned counterpane that some one had offered, telling them to stand ready for whatever might happen.

"Come closer, boys," said one of them, wetting his hat in a tub of water: "if we take a little scorchin' doin' this now, we may git it cooler in the next world!"

"Amen! Trust the Lord!" said the cobbler; and just then Marm Lisa appeared at one of the top windows with a child in her arms. No one else could have recognized Atlantic in the smoke, but Rhoda and Mary knew the round cropped head and the familiar blue gingham apron.

Lisa stood in the empty window-frame, a trembling figure on a background of flame. Her post was not at the moment in absolute danger. There was hope yet, though to the onlookers there seemed none.

"Throw him!" "Drop him!" "Le' go of him!" shouted the crowd.

"Hold your jaws, and let me do the talking!" roared the policeman. "Stop your noise, if you don't want two dead children on your consciences! Keep back, you brutes, keep back o' the rope, or I'll club you!"

It was not so much the officer's threats as simple, honest awe that caused a sudden hush to fall. There were whispering, sighs, tears, murmurings, but all so subdued that it seemed like silence in the midst of the fierce crackling of the flames.

"Drop him! We'll ketch him in the quilt!" called the policeman, standing as near as he dared.

Lisa looked shudderingly at the desperate

means of salvation so far below, and, turn-
ing her face away as much as she could,
unclasped her arms despairingly, and Atlantic came swooping down from their shelter,
down, down into the counterpane; stunned,
stifled, choked by smoke, but uninjured, as
Lisa knew by the cheers that greeted his
safe descent.

A tongue of fire curled round the corner
of the building and ran up to the roof towards another that was licking its way along
the top of the window.

"Jump now yourself!" called the policeman, while two more men silently joined
the four holding the corners of the quilt.
Every eye was fixed on the motionless figure
of Marm Lisa, who had drawn her shawl
over her head, as if just conscious of nearer
heat.

The wind changed, and blew the smoke
away from her figure. The men on the
roof stopped work, not caring for the moment whether they saved the tenement house
or not, since a human life was hanging in
the balance. The intoxicated woman threw
a beer-bottle into the street, and her son ran
up from the crowd and locked her safely in
her kitchen at the back of the house.

"Jump this minute, or you're a dead girl!" shouted the officer, hoarse with emotion. "God A'mighty, she ain't goin' to jump, — she's terror-struck! She'll burn right there before our eyes, when we could climb up and drag her down if we had a long enough ladder!"

"They've found another ladder, and are tying two together," somebody said.

"The fire company's comin'! I hear 'em!" cried somebody else.

"They'll be too late," moaned Rhoda, "too late! Oh, Mary, make her jump!"

Lisa had felt no fear while she darted through smoke and over charred floors in pursuit of Atlantic, — no fear, nothing but joy when she dragged him out from under a bench and climbed to the window-sill with him, — but now that he was saved she seemed paralyzed. So still she was she might have been a carven statue save for the fluttering of the garments about her thin childish legs. The distance to the ground looked impassable, and she could not collect her thoughts for the hissing of the flame as it ate up the floor in the room behind her. Horrible as it was, she thought it would be easier to let it steal behind her and wrap her in its burning embrace than to drop from these dizzy heights down through that terrible distance to hear her own bones snap as she touched the quilt, and to see her own blood staining the ground.

"She 'll burn, sure," said a man. " Well, she 's half witted, — that 's one comfort!"

Mary started as if she were stung, and forced her way still nearer to the window, hoping to gain a position where she could be more plainly seen.

Everybody thought something was going to happen. Mary had dozens of friends and more acquaintances in that motley assemblage, and they somehow felt that there were dramatic possibilities in the situation. Unless she could think of something, Marm Lisa's last chance was gone: that was the sentiment of the crowd, and Mary agreed in it.

Her cape had long since dropped from her shoulders, her hat was trampled under foot, the fair coil of hair had loosened and was falling on her neck, and the steel fillet blazed in the firelight. She stepped to the quilt and made a despairing movement to attract Lisa's attention.

"Li-sa!" she called, in that sweet, carrying woman's voice that goes so much farther than a man's.

The child started, and, pushing back the shawl, looked out from under its cover, her head raised, her eyes brightening.

Mary chanced all on that one electrical moment of recognition, and, with a mien half commanding and half appealing, she stretched out both her arms and called again, while the crowd held its breath: "Come to me, darling! Jump, little sister! *Now!*"

Not one second did Marm Lisa hesitate. She would have sprung into the fire at that dear mandate, and, closing her eyes, she leaped into the air as the roof above her head fell in with a crash.

Just then the beating of hoofs and jangling of bells in the distance announced the coming of the belated firemen; not so long belated actually, for all the emotions, heart-beats, terrors, and despairs that go to make up tragedy can be lived through in a few brief moments.

In that sudden plunge from window to earth Marm Lisa seemed to die consciously. The gray world, the sad world, vanished, "and the immortal light, all young and joy-

ful, million-orbed, million-colored," beamed
on her darkness. She kept on falling, falling, falling, till she reached the abysmal
depths of space, — then she knew no more:
and Mary, though prone on the earth, kept
falling, falling, falling with her into so deep
a swoon that she woke only to find herself
on a friendly bed, with Rhoda, and Lisa
herself, weeping over her.

At five o'clock, Mrs. Grubb, forcibly torn
from a meeting and acquainted with the afternoon's proceedings, hurried into a lower
room in the tenement house, where Mary,
Rhoda, and the three children were gathered
for a time. There were still a hundred
people in the street, but they showed their
respect by keeping four or five feet away
from the windows.

The twins sat on a sofa, more quiet than
anything save death itself. They had been
rocked to the very centre of their being,
and looked like nothing so much as a couple
of faded photographs of themselves. Lisa
lay on a cot, sleeping restlessly; Mary
looked pale and wan, and there were dark
circles under her eyes.

As Mrs. Grubb opened the door softly,
Mary rose to meet her.

"Have you heard all?" she asked.

"Yes, everything!" faltered Mrs. Grubb, with quivering lips and downcast eyelids.

Mary turned towards Lisa's bed. "Mrs. Grubb," she said, looking straight into that lady's clear, shallow eyes, "I think Lisa has earned her freedom, and I the right to ask a Christmas gift of you. Stand on the other side of the cot, and put your hand in mine. I ask you for the last time, will you give this unfinished, imperfect life into my keeping, if I promise to be faithful to it unto the end, whatever it may be?"

I suppose that every human creature, be he ever so paltry, has his hour of effulgence, an hour when the mortal veil grows thin and the divine image stands revealed, endowing him, for a brief space at least, with a kind of awful beauty and majesty.

It was Mistress Mary's hour. Her pure, unswerving spirit shone with a white and steady radiance that illuminated Mrs. Grubb's soul to its very depths, showing her in a flash the feeble flickerings and waverings of her own trivial purposes. At that moment her eye was fitted with a new lens, through which the road to the summit of the Tehachapi Mountains and Mahat-

madom suddenly looked long, weary, and
profitless, and by means of which the twins
were transferred from the comfortable middle distance they had previously occupied to
the immediate foreground of duty. The
lens might slip, but while it was in place
she saw as clearly as another woman.

"Will you?" repeated Mistress Mary,
wondering at her silence.

Mrs. Grubb gave one last glance at the
still reproach of Lisa's face, and one more
at the twins, who seemed to loom more for-
midably each time she regarded them; then
drawing a deep breath, she said, "Yes, I
will; I *will*, no matter what happens; —
but it is n't enough to give up, and you
need n't suppose I think it is." And taking a passive twin by either hand, she passed
out of the door into the crowded thorough-
fare, and disappeared in the narrow streets
that led to Eden Place.